y mum

D0458549

09 JAN 2009

Miles from Nowhere

Miles from Nowhere

Nami Mun

Riverhead Books

a member of Penguin Group (USA) Inc

New York   2009

RIVERHEAD BOOKS
Published by the Penguin Group
Penguin Group (USA) Inc., 375 Hudson Street, New York, New York 10014,
USA • Penguin Group (Canada), 90 Eglinton Avenue East, Suite 700, Toronto,
Ontario M4P 2Y3, Canada (a division of Pearson Canada Inc.) • Penguin Books Ltd,
80 Strand, London WC2R 0RL, England • Penguin Ireland, 25 St Stephen's Green,
Dublin 2, Ireland (a division of Penguin Books Ltd) • Penguin Group (Australia),
250 Camberwell Road, Camberwell, Victoria 3124, Australia
(a division of Pearson Australia Group Pty Ltd) • Penguin Books India Pvt Ltd,
11 Community Centre, Panchsheel Park, New Delhi–110 017, India • Penguin
Group (NZ), 67 Apollo Drive, Rosedale, North Shore 0632, New Zealand
(a division of Pearson New Zealand Ltd) • Penguin Books (South Africa) (Pty)
Ltd, 24 Sturdee Avenue, Rosebank, Johannesburg 2196, South Africa

Penguin Books Ltd, Registered Offices: 80 Strand, London WC2R 0RL, England

Library of Congress Cataloging-in-Publication Data

Mun, Nami.
Miles from nowhere / Nami Mun.
p.   cm.
ISBN 978-1-59448-854-2
1. Teenage girls—Fiction.   2. Runaway teenagers—Fiction.
3. New York (N.Y.)—Fiction.   4. Psychological fiction.   I. Title.
PS3613.U4565M56   2009   2008018815
813'.6—dc22

Printed in the United States of America
1   3   5   7   9   10   8   6   4   2

Book design by Claire Naylon Vaccaro

This is a work of fiction. Names, characters, places, and incidents either are
the product of the author's imagination or are used fictitiously, and any
resemblance to actual persons, living or dead, businesses, companies,
events, or locales is entirely coincidental.

While the author has made every effort to provide accurate telephone numbers
and Internet addresses at the time of publication, neither the publisher nor the author
assumes any responsibility for errors, or for changes that occur after publication.
Further, the publisher does not have any control over and does not assume any
responsibility for author or third-party websites or their content.

For Gus, my believer

Contents

To see clearly and without flinching,
without turning away,
this is agony, the eyes taped open
two inches from the sun.

—*Margaret Atwood,*
NOTES TOWARDS A POEM
THAT CAN NEVER BE WRITTEN

Shelter

I'd been at the shelter for two weeks and there was nothing to do but go to counseling or lie on my cot and count the rows of empty cots nailed to the floor or watch TV in the rec room, where the girls cornrowed each other's hair and went on about pulling a date with Reggie the counselor because he looked like Billy Dee Williams and had a rump-roast ass. I didn't see a way to join in, but I didn't feel like being alone, either. It was cold. Outside the lobby doors, the thick snow falling made it hard to see the diner across the street. The walls in this place were too bright, too lit up in a peppermint light. I wandered down the long hallway, walked past the cafeteria and the nurses' station without saying hi to anyone, and looked for Knowledge.

I liked Knowledge. She'd stood up for me my first night—whacked a huge girl across her face with a dinner tray and then plunked right down on top of her. With a hand choking the girl's neck, Knowledge told her to give back my sneakers because that was the right thing to do. I actually hated those sneakers, was glad when the girl stole them so the counselors could give me a new pair, but that really wasn't the point. Nobody had ever stuck up for me before.

I saw Knowledge at the end of the hall, jumping rope.

"Okay, how about this," she said as I walked up. "What if I was to pull off something really big, something that'll change our lives forever, but I needed your help. You gonna be there?" The rope buzzed over her face as her eyes focused on some point down the hallway.

"Depends," I said, hopping an imaginary hopscotch. "You want to go play cards?"

"*Depends*? On what?" She stopped jumping. The white beads in her hair stopped jumping, too. Clenching the rope, she said, "You either trust me or you don't. We're either partners or we ain't, and believe me, you can't make it on the street without a partner covering your flat ass." She yanked up her gloves, which were really tube socks with ten finger holes. "So, you'd watch my back or what?"

"If I say okay, can we go play cards?"

"Good. That's what I'm talking about. Here, take this."

I took the rope from her and she dropped to the floor. Between each push-up, she bubbled her cheeks and exhaled real loud. "Gotta get in shape so we can bust out tonight."

I coiled the rope around my wrist to make an African tribal bracelet. I didn't know what she was talking about, and plus, the shelter doors were always open—we could leave whenever we wanted. Over the speakers, dinner was being announced.

"C'mon. Let's go," I said. "I'll let you teach me blackjack."

"At a time like this? You gotta be out of your mind." She shot up and began running fast in place, slowing down only to deliver uppercuts.

My mom turned crazy the night my father left us for good. He had given up on us. On my mother's ways. She was getting up in the middle of the night and stepping out onto our cold, muddy yard to dig a hole in the ground. Every night for a week she worked on that one hole, as if trying to tunnel her way back to Korea. It had been her idea to move us to the States four years before, and my dad never let her forget it.

I was twelve then. It was winter. Her small spade hitting the dirt sounded like coughing.

That night, as soon as my dad's car turned the corner, she dropped the spade and turned to me. I felt the eyes of the neighborhood wives and grandmothers peeking through blinds and curtains, judging us, wondering if people like us deserved to share their skies. A gust of wind brought my mom's hair to life and, even though I knew words were coming from her mouth, it seemed as if the black, uncombed strands were the ones speaking. She ordered me to grab all of his things and pile them in our yard. Like his socks, underwear, toothbrush, the basement TV, his leather Bible, the briefcase I'd gotten him for his birthday which he never used, pictures of him, pictures of him and me, his half-empty jar of Sanka. While I made runs back and forth, my mom lay on the dead grass, the moon shining down on her tears and the small pile of Dad I'd created next to her. She rolled her

4

face to the side, her ear touching dirt. "What do you think God does to people like you?" she asked the ground.

She had on only her robe, and no socks. She was naked underneath. I asked her if she was cold. Without answering, she stood up, slapped something off her knees, and stared past me and into the house. "Did you grab everything?"

I nodded and looked down at the slippers he'd bought me, wondering if they were supposed to go into the pile. Before I could ask, she walked off into the garage and came out seconds later carrying a small can in each hand. With all the lighter fluid, the pile lit up fast, the flash instantly warming my face. I stood there and didn't try to stop her because I loved her too much then. I knew it wasn't good to burn all of Dad's things, but how can you not love someone who lets you see them in all that pain? For the first time, I saw her clearly, as if I were inside a dream of hers, watching all her thoughts. She wasn't putting on an act. She wasn't being a nurse. She wasn't being a mother or a wife or a good Christian. She was just dropping to her knees, inches from the fire, and sliding her thin arms into the flames. If I screamed I didn't hear it, but I did pull her back, grabbing a fistful of her bathrobe, fully understanding that I was now playing a part in that dream.

When the fire trucks and the ambulance came, I left her and ran into the house. I locked all the doors, turned off all the lights because we had revealed too much of ourselves. Crouching under a window that faced the yard, I heard two neighbors saying how they'd never seen such a thing. A man asked my mom how she felt.

All she said was, "I'm starving."

In the cafeteria, Knowledge said to me, "Life's only as bad as you make it out to be. It's got nothing to do with the way it is." After three quick shovels of mashed potatoes, she mumbled, "You get me?" Her knees rattled under our table. I folded and unfolded the paper napkin on my lap and drank my milk before telling her that I didn't, and that I didn't understand most of what she said.

She nodded. "I like your honesty. I do. I demand it, actually," she said, and patted my back. "Here, for your bones." From under her sweatshirt she pulled out a half-pint of milk and sneaked it onto my lap. "You know, I never knew a Chink before."

"That's okay." I packed the mash and the Salisbury steak inside my dinner roll.

"I didn't even know Chinks ran away from home."

"We can do a lot of neat things," I said, swallowing. I liked hearing her laugh. And I didn't care that she'd called me a Chink, though I wanted to say that Chinks were for Chinese and that Koreans had their own special name. But that was another subject, and I liked the way we were talking right then.

"Hello, ladies."

I'd seen Wink walk up to us—strutting past the tables, looking to see who was checking him out. He could've been Chachi's younger brother, dressed in tight jeans with a red bandanna tied around his thigh.

Knowledge pointed her plastic fork at him and yelled, "Don't even start aiming your ass for the bench." She didn't like boys talking to me, especially Wink. To her, boys were either weak or evil—and Wink was both.

"You're the boss," he said, and sat down next to me anyway. I admired that about him. He could really annoy people, but at least he was stubborn about it. And he didn't seem to care what anyone said behind his back, even after the whole counseling incident. I only got the story from Knowledge, but during Wink's first rap session, some guys I guess sobbed and told their runaway stories, and when it was Wink's turn, he admitted that he'd been on the streets for almost a year because his mom used to heat up a coat hanger and beat him with it when he was little. Then she was sent to Bellevue for trying to hang herself *and* him. Anyway, he cried, too. After the session ended and the counselor left, the boys cornered Wink and pushed him down, stepping on him and laughing. They told him that they'd all made up their stories, and how they rolled queers like him for kicks. Knowledge then told me that Wink was a prostitute, that he was whoring before he came to the shelter and he sure as hell was gonna be whoring after he left. I didn't even know they had boy prostitutes.

You couldn't tell any of this by looking at him, though. Always in his shiny Members Only jacket with the sleeves scrunched up, Wink walked around the place like he was the president of money.

"Hey," he said, just to me. "I wanna show you something." He took out a baseball from his jacket pocket, and I was about to take a closer look when Knowledge elbowed me in the ribs. "Don't tell him about tonight," she whispered.

"What about tonight?" I whispered back. She just waved her hand and shushed me.

Then Wink said something.

"What?" I turned to him.

"It's autographed, see?"

He propped the baseball against my tray. Big capital letters, spelling out WILLIE MAYS, slithered across the ball, every letter strung together like some penmanship exercise. I could tell he wanted me to pick up the ball and say something nice about it, but from my right side I felt Knowledge's eyes burning a hole in my cheek.

"Hey, you gonna be here on Christmas?" Wink asked, taking back the ball.

I told him that I didn't know. With a spoon, I mashed my mashed potatoes and tried my best to feel comfortable sitting between these two.

"That's cool because..." Wink juggled the baseball from one hand to the other. "Because I got you a gift."

"Oh." I bit into my sandwich.

"And I'm telling you so you have time to get me one," he said, and laughed a little.

"Don't you know it's rude to whisper?" Knowledge thwacked the back of his head, which made Wink jump out of his seat.

"Don't touch me, you crazy dyke." He pulled his arm back, looking to beam the ball at her. Knowledge didn't flinch. She just stood up, bumped her chest into his, and stared him down. "Jesus fuck," he said. "Why can't you act like a girl for once?"

A few kids had gathered around us. "A fight, a fight, a nigga and a white," one girl sang but we all knew Wink would back down. Beat up a girl or get beaten by a girl, either way, it didn't look good.

"This is bunk, man. I'm outta here." He tucked the baseball back into his jacket pocket. "I'll see you later, my Korean empress," he said, and gave me a wink. As he swaggered out of the cafeteria, practically all the girls booed him, calling him a white ass honky trick baby.

It was lights-out at ten. Knowledge slept in the cot next to mine and, as usual, she cried in her sleep. I got to know her best during these times. On most nights, she called out to someone, and by the way her lips trembled, you could tell the person never came. I thought about who this person could be, and I thought about my mom, how heavy her eyes had looked the night my father left, how her bathrobe smelled like gasoline. After the sirens faded and the neighbors went back into their homes, I rummaged through our house all over again, this time to see if my father had left me a note. Or maybe a phone number. Nothing turned up. The house was quiet for the first time in months. I dragged my blanket into the living room and watched TV, but mostly I kept thinking somebody would call—the cops or the hospital. No one did. I did see our next-door neighbor Mr. McCommon pacing his driveway with eyes to the ground. He didn't come by, either. I didn't feel sad or lonely, just numb. I opened up a package of dry instant noodles, dipped chunks of it in peanut butter, and stayed up late to watch *Midnight Kung Fu Theater*.

Knowledge mumbled something. I rolled to my side to look at her—her short thick lashes upcurled so tight. I liked watching her like this—I liked that there was nothing between me and her. Not even her. But then she scrunched her brows, which made her look more scared than usual.

"Hey." I leaned over and nudged her arm.

She opened her eyes really big and didn't blink.

"Did it seem real?" I lay back down, ready to hear out her dream, ready to fall asleep to it.

"Get up," she said. "It's time." She sat up and launched her legs into her pants.

"Time for sleep, right?"

"Hey, you trust me or what?"

"Not really," I said. Knowledge didn't laugh, though. She was too busy putting on her T-shirt—her head popping up first, then both arms sprouting out together.

"Okay, this is what's gonna happen. I'll cause a distraction. But you gotta get past the Pigs by yourself, all right?"

"What pigs?"

"And you gotta hurry, Joon."

I sat up. "What's happening to your brain right now?"

She rolled her eyes in disgust. "Just look around the room, idiot."

I looked around. Four walls. A piano nobody touched. Rows of green cots, each with a lump of a girl.

"Do I gotta say more?" she asked, making her bed.

"If you want me to understand you."

"Exactly." She shot a look at the door. Her eyes were working so hard solving some geometry problem in her head, it seemed more dangerous to interrupt her.

"Wait for me at the Greek's across the street. You got until the count of five. *That's* your distraction."

"Distraction for what?" I asked, but she was already sprinting out of the room, screaming, "One! Two! Three! Four! Five!"

Outside, I could hear her running back and forth, yelling, "Deck the halls with boughs of holly!" like she was demanding you to do it.

"Crazy ass motherfucker," a voice said in the dark.

I got dressed.

In the front lobby, Reggie sat with his feet up on the desk, the toothpick in his mouth twirling a little as he mumbled into the phone. I considered waving goodbye to him but decided to just go. He probably didn't even know who I was.

"Your bed ain't gonna be here when you come back," he said, covering the mouthpiece. He really did look like Billy Dee Williams.

With some drama, I hipped the door open and flashed him a look that said, "Oh well." The snow hadn't let up. I tucked my sweatshirt into my jeans and crossed the street. I'd forgotten about the bed policy, but who cared. That was what Knowledge would've said, or something more fortune cookie–like, like, *The bed belongs to no one.*

With no money for the diner, I waited outside and watched people walk by in their long black coats, hats over ears, their lips blowing smoke. Some people ran and ducked into cabs, their bodies swallowed up in one gulp. Others vanished in sections, inch by inch, as they stepped down the subway stairs. Then there were the people up the block whose bodies turned to black strings until they thinned out of sight. All these people, rushing through the streets as if something good waited for them back home. Inside the diner, President Carter was waving from an airplane until an old waiter climbed up onto the counter and clicked the TV off. The waiter then shuffled around, flicking off the lights with the crook of his cane. Somehow, the diner going dark made the sidewalk seem colder. A diner. That was what my mom had wanted to open our first year here, a Korean one. She told us she would waitress, I would work the register after school, and my dad would have to cook because of his English. When she got to this part of her plan, my dad grabbed her wrists. "Who do you think you are, telling me to work in a kitchen," he said, strangling her tiny bones.

The old waiter came out and slammed the door behind him. In a thick accent he shouted that he was closing up, and shooed me away so he could pull the gate shut. I stepped aside. The stubble on his face looked like snowflakes. "She'll be here any second," I assured him.

"I am very happy for you," he said, and yanked on the padlock to make sure it had fastened.

That's when I saw Wink. Zipping up his jacket, he strolled out of the shelter and casually jogged across the street toward me. I stopped myself from running to him, and for that long second he was my best friend.

"I thought you weren't gonna leave," he said, giving me a hug. I was surprised by the hugging thing, but it felt okay. We let go quick.

"Knowledge has some kind of . . . a plan," I told him.

"Man, she stinks of trouble." Wink was already shivering, blowing into his cupped hands. "She doesn't care about nothing but *her*self, and *her* shit, and— Excuse me! Excuse me, sir! Can you spare some change so me and my little sister could get something to eat?"

A man bustling by stopped to search his coat pocket. While digging for money, he glanced at me, and then at Wink, who kept his head down. "You two are related, that's what you're telling me, right?" The man handed over some coins anyway.

Wink saluted. "Thank you, sir. My sister thanks you, too." As the man walked off, Wink counted the money. "Twelve cents?" he shouted. "You fucking dick!"

He seemed different outside the shelter, older maybe.

Even his eyes looked darker. I wondered about Knowledge, if she would look older, too. I didn't have to wonder for too long, though.

Knowledge bolted through the shelter doors, screaming, "We made it!" and charged the street as if she'd just barely escaped an explosion. Behind her, Reggie swiveled in his chair with his back to us, still on the phone.

"We made it!" she hollered again, putting her hand on my arm, and I thought she wanted to lean on me so she could rest but instead she hauled me across the street, stopping traffic, and practically tossed me down into the subway.

The train rocked us from side to side.

"Who the fuck invited you?" she yelled.

"Ah, shut up. You're just pissed 'cause you ain't got a dick."

"I'm still more man than you, you skanky fag."

"Hey, guys?" I said, mostly to myself, which was why I was surprised when they both actually stopped shouting. "Do we know where we're going?"

Knowledge tapped her chest. "You leave that to me," she said, and propped her legs on the seat in front of us.

Wink stood by the doors with his arms folded and feet apart. "I ain't a queer," was all he said.

The tracks made a dry, whistling sound.

"Give me your shoelaces," Knowledge told us, and started untying hers.

Wink and I shared a look.

"Do you even know what a freak you are? I ain't giving you my laces or anything like my laces," he said, and turned to me. "Joon. What're you doing?"

"Giving her my laces."

"Why?"

Because it was easier to do what others wanted. And quieter. I didn't say this to Wink, though. I just shrugged.

A few stops later, a black man carrying a McDonald's bag came on, and our car instantly smelled of fries. He looked tired. The light behind his eyes had been turned off for the night. I liked him because of his construction boots—the mud on them made me believe he was hardworking and honest. After taking a seat in the middle of the car, he bit into his burger, stared down at it while chewing, and then looked out the window, which only gave back a darker version of him. At the end of the car, another man sat by himself, too, but him I didn't like, especially his mustache the size of a rat. The skin on his face was too tight and too shiny, as if you could peel it off and find underneath a skull made of porcelain. Plus, when we'd first hopped on the train, he cinched up his overcoat and glared at us, as if we were looking to steal his kidneys.

I wouldn't have noticed this man again except that Wink was now walking up to him, dragging his sneakers a little since having given up his laces. He grabbed the top rail and dangled his body in front of the man's face, pretending to read an ad, while the man slowly stroked his mustache, pretending not to see him.

Knowledge plopped down next to me. "You seeing this? What did I tell you?" She shook her head and gave a few tut-tuts while braiding all of our laces into one long rope. Green gems of light streaked the windows as our train went through what seemed like an endless tunnel, and Knowledge babbled about sex being a weakness and how all men were sick with this disease. The man stood up, and Wink led him toward the next car. "If you can't control yourself, something else will," Knowledge said, and I secretly wished for her to shut up. Using all his weight, Wink jerked open the sliding door and walked on through without looking back.

Shelter

.   .   .

We shot out of the tunnel and all the sounds of the train turned loose in the air. I took a breath. The subway had turned into an El, and the shaky tracks reminded me of a tired roller coaster. Down below, dark bodies in fat hooded jackets walked by tenements. Some buildings were empty, some burned black. One had pretty flower planters on every windowsill, with a little white boy or a little black girl staring out and smiling stupidly from every window. But everyone knew the kids weren't real—they were the fake window posters the city had pasted up. The front of our train curved into an S, and just like that, the streets disappeared and the apartment buildings were now only inches away. We moved slowly, and each family's window clicked by like View-Master frames. They were so close, I could've touched every one of them—the man and his kids watching TV, the big-breasted aproned mother tying up a garbage bag, and then a girl my age talking on the phone, ignoring the Christmas tree standing right beside her. It was too cold to pull down the window but I did it anyway. I wanted to put my face out there and smell every home.

. . .

When my mother came back from the hospital, she wouldn't speak to me. She wouldn't even look at me. After a few days of silence, I tried shocking her into talking—I chopped off my hair, played Meat Loaf really loud, stared at her without blinking while she prayed by her bed, but nothing. She eventually spent her days locked in her room, and I hung out at a diner near our house, sipping Mello Yello at the counter, eavesdropping on conversations long enough until I felt I could join in. My mom and I only saw each other once in a while, in the kitchen or the hallway. We ate alone, we cried alone, we didn't answer the door. My dad never called.

One night I found her reading her Bible on the sofa. I sat next to her and begged her to say one word, just one. I even gave her some suggestions: Apple. Lotion. Jesus. Rice. She didn't look up from the pages.

This lasted six months. This lasted until the day I left.

Our train stayed in the station awhile with all the doors open. By the stairs I waited for Wink. He stood with his back against a platform column, talking to the man without touching him. The snow kept falling. It was hard to tell if he knew we were waiting for him, and I didn't think I could interrupt. Knowledge was jogging up and down the subway stairs, losing her patience. "We got things to do," she said during her fifth lap, and I couldn't blame her. She tugged the elbow of my sweatshirt, gentler than I'd expected, and we walked down the steps and out onto Tremont Avenue.

I looked up at the sky, and at the little snow-guppies swimming in streaks of light. It was colder here than in the city, not enough tall buildings blocking the wind. My jeans, crusty and cold, scraped against the skin of my thighs as we walked beside a row of double-parked cars, passed fire escapes ringed with bicycle wheels and windows draped with towels and pillowcases. A long car without headlights floated by in darkness. Across the street a small dog raised its leg and the wind blew its pee onto a liquor store sign that advertised CHICKEN LIVER & HOT CHOCOLATE $2.35.

Knowledge marched with hands in her pockets, her shoulders hunched, her face chiseled with determination.

"Do you think you'll ever tell me where we're going?" I asked.

She stopped short and put a hand on my arm. "You should trust me more."

"Okay."

She squeezed harder. "No, I mean it. We can't be friends if you don't trust me."

"I said okay."

"Okay you trust me or okay you don't want to be friends?"

"Okay I trust you, but it's really cold."

"What's that got to do with anything?"

My face felt like a crackling mask. "Can't we just get to where we need to go?"

"Sure," she said, whipping out the rope she'd made from our laces. "But we're already here."

We'd stopped in front of a building, under a fire escape ladder. She tossed the rope up several times. When it finally lassoed the bottom rung, she tugged on the ends of the rope until the ladder squealed and slid down a few inches. Without saying a word, she put on her sock-gloves, stepped back about five paces, took a running leap, and just barely caught the bottom rung with the tips of her fingers. "Pull me," she said, after securing her grip, and I hugged her knees and pulled, which drew the ladder down the rest of the way.

I looked down the street, in both directions, searching for something or someone to decide for me. The sidewalk was empty, except for an empty potato chip bag skidding toward me with the wind. I could see the train tracks, but I didn't see Wink. I wanted to look for him, but I wasn't sure if he wanted to be found. I understood this, the difference between getting lost and staying lost. I had left home to bring back my father, and when my search failed, I knew that meant that he wanted to stay gone. Which made me sad. And then jealous of his freedom. So I stayed gone, too, and left my mom to live alone, inside that tunnel of grief. I didn't even go back to say goodbye.

"Pssst!" Knowledge waved me up from the third floor.

By the time I caught up to her, she was trying to open a window.

"It's unlocked," she said. "Help me get it open."

I got next to her and the two of us looked like weight lifters—our knees bent, our hands by our ears, straining to lift up a window that wouldn't budge. I felt queasy. I knew this was wrong. "Can you please tell me what we're doing?"

23

"You'll see," she said, and right then, the window burst open. A gust of snowflakes rushed inside, and before I could say a word, she slinked in.

I stepped onto a table, then down to a chair, then to a floor that creaked when I landed. The kitchen smelled of fish grease. It was dark but not so black that I couldn't see Knowledge opening the refrigerator. She poked her head in and turned to me, pinching her nose and shaking her head. How she could even think about food, I didn't understand. I was sick to my stomach—my whole body felt heavier, muddier, sneaking around someone else's home. I heard every sound I made as I followed her across a hallway and into a room that was blinking red, white, red, white.

And then I saw it, what she had wanted me to see— a humongous white Christmas tree that was as tall as the ceiling and as big as the tree at Alexander's department store. Knowledge stood with her hands on her hips, studying every Santa head and every strand of silver tinsel clumped on the plastic branches. The flashing lights changed the color of her face, and she smiled up at the tree as if the black angel perched on top were singing secrets. I didn't see any presents, though. Not under the tree or anywhere else in the living room, which was crowded sets. Above the couch hung a poster-sized photo of a black couple. The woman had thick pretty lashes and sat with her hands folded on her lap. Behind her stood a stocky man with tinted glasses and Jheri curls, wearing a velvet suit. The picture made him look as though he had only one hand—a fat one, with a gold pinkie ring, resting on the woman's thin shoulder. I was about to point the poster out to Knowledge when I saw that she was under the tree.

"Don't worry," she whispered, "it's lighter than you think."

She was bent over, picking the tree up by the stand and telling me to grab the top.

"Are you crazy?" I checked behind me.

"Just shut up and help me," she whisper-shouted.

Right then a light came on down the hallway. I didn't even think—I ran. And for some reason I thought Knowledge would, too. With one foot out the window, I turned back to find her dragging the tree into the kitchen, stand and all. I begged her to let go of it but knew she wouldn't listen, so I helped her, and we had almost half the tree shoved out onto the fire escape when the kitchen light came on.

It was the man from the photo, only much thicker. I hadn't expected him to come out wearing a velvet suit or anything, but I was surprised to see him in his black socks and tiny underwear, his beefy stomach large enough to house the woman standing next to him. She stood with her hands covering her nose and mouth, like she was about to cough.

"Knowledge," the woman finally said.

The three of them stood frozen. The woman, with a pink curler in her bangs, stared at Knowledge. The man, with his arms folded, stared at the tree. And Knowledge, unable to face either of them, stared at the refrigerator. Me: I couldn't believe Knowledge was her real name.

"Let's go," she said suddenly, and pushed the tree out the window. She didn't care about the ornaments anymore. The angel had fallen off by the hallway.

As soon as we got outside, we tossed the tree over the railing, watched it land in the middle of the street, and scrambled down the fire escape.

"She'll be back. You watch. You'll be back!" the man shouted, his head out the window. I kept waiting to hear the woman's voice but it never came. We jumped down to the sidewalk. "And what, you think I'm just gonna give you my damn tree?" the man went on.

didn't give it to me, asshole. I took it from you. She propped the tree up and started skipping around it, singing, "I took it, I took it, I took it, and I ain't gonna take it anymore!"

An old lady on the second floor poked her head out and threatened to come down and wring our necks with her own bare hands, so help her God.

"You know why you'll be back?" the man started again. "Who the hell would want you? You're too damn ugly to get anyone else. Look at her, she don't even look like a—"

A blur of white flew over the man's head right then and shattered his window. The sound of glass breaking was so clear, almost cartoonish. Knowledge and I both turned to see Wink across the street, smiling at his aim.

"C'mon!" Knowledge screamed, and Wink snapped to. He ran toward us, now laughing, and only then did I see he was carrying a paper bag.

"Shermaine, call the police," the man yelled, and, as if we were of one body, the three of us grabbed the tree at the exact same time—Knowledge in front, me in the middle, and Wink with a free hand holding up the base—and we ran as if a gun had gone off and a race had started. The cold air bit my nose, and my sneakers felt as if they might slip off any second, but by the end of the block we were laughing. Wink hollered, "Merry Christmas, I love you all," over and over again while Knowledge screamed, "Fuck you, barbershop. Fuck you, butcher. Fuck you, basketball court and playground," just fuck you to every place we ran past. Leaving a trail of Santa heads behind us, Knowledge sped us through the neighborhood. "Look at them fools, running with a damn tree," a skinny old man said, standing in front of the liquor store. "Fuck you, old man," Knowledge shouted. And with the snow hitting my eyes, my fingers almost numb, I suddenly felt like one of those people who walked the streets as if something good were waiting for them.

We turned a corner and ran across an entire square block that looked to have been bombed. I'd seen it from the El. Piles and piles of rubble, of broken buildings. We trampled over bricks, cement blocks, toilet bowls, and tire rims until we finally rushed into a tall, burned-out building. "Up here," Knowledge said, tugging on the tree, and we followed her to the third floor and into a room.

The room was big. We dropped the tree in the center. We didn't know what to do first, laugh or catch our breath, so we did both, and hugged and gave each other high fives, saying, "Aw man, that was the fucking best and things like that and looked up at the tall empty tree, which seemed so different in this room. The floor was covered in sheets of newspaper, cereal boxes, liquor bottles, and dried shit. A burned mattress with spirals poking through took up a corner, and the wall beside it had a hole the size of a small car that let us see where we'd come from. Wink opened up his paper bag, which was now soggy, and, to our surprise, he handed out Styrofoam cups. Knowledge peeled the lid off and took a sip. It was hot chocolate. And not even Ovaltine, but the real thing, with whipped cream and sprinkles, at least that's the way I remember it. "Goddamn! This is good, isn't it?" Wink shouted, almost searing me. He peeled the room and took sips, one right after another. "You know what it tastes like?" He touched his chest, right where his heart was, and scrunched his jacket. "It tastes like love," he said, and fell to the ground, pretending to have been shot. I laughed and dropped down next to him, and then Knowledge next to me. "Tastes like love, my ass," she said.

In the new quiet we heard the El crawling by, the sound reminding me of Wink and that man, and it wasn't until the train left us for good that we realized Wink was crying. He wiped his nose across his arm and took a long sip from his cup. I imagined a lump in his throat being washed over. I drank, too, wanting to taste whatever he tasted, and soon our breathing slowed and we sat there, our numbness wearing off, not really knowing what else to say, and not seeing the room or the walls or the sky outside or even one another, but only seeing the tree in front of us, for exactly what it was.

Nothing About Love or Pity

They were trying to crack my face in two. It didn't make sense. They punched me, across the nose, up the cheek, in my ear. The back of my head struck ground, reminding me that I had a skull. I couldn't talk. A face hovered above me. Large teeth. Slippery hair. Puffy coat. Hands pinned my shoulders and legs to the ground even though I'd given up fighting. It was still snowing. It was always snowing. *Hurry up*, a voice said. Then someone was laughing. Someone was singing. Someone was pulling down my pants. Their fingers metal cold. *I'm thirteen*, I said, and other ridiculous words. I heard me begging. It didn't sound like me. It sounded like an old lady whispering in a cave. Someone kicked my words back in, and instantly, I saw my dad, slapping me in the parking lot behind our church. It didn't matter. I wanted my dad to suddenly appear and save me. It seemed like a fair request. *Please*, I said, and took another punch. This time there was no telling where it landed. My brain felt broken. It stopped sending messages. I was trapped in my body, and my body was trapped in this empty lot with men who knew nothing about love or pity but everything else crucial. That I was lost. That I trusted strangers. That I needed to be taught a lesson. Knowledge was right. I wouldn't make it on the streets on my own.

And then, everything froze. I wondered if I had somehow stopped time. I heard their breathing, I even heard them squinting, and soon we were drenched in a light so white I thought the moon had exploded. A car honked its horn, scaring the guy off me. The rest of them ran like drunk roaches, the slush of their footsteps melting into memory. And just like that, they were all gone.

It took a few years for them to really leave.

I reached down. My underwear was still on. They hadn't ruined me. At least not in that way. *Life's only as bad as you make it out to be. It's got nothing to do with the way it is.* The blood in my mouth was overflowing. I wanted to spit but was afraid to move my head, so I swallowed, letting in a queasiness that didn't feel all bad.

"You all right?"

It was a man's voice. He put a hand on my chin and turned my head to him. A black man with a white beard. "You're okay," he said, trying to convince me. "I'm okay," I said, laughing a little, needing to prove something about myself. He took off his parka and covered me. I looked at him harder, this time in little chunks. A bald head, an anchor-shaped nose, thick glasses that magnified everything behind them. He looked nothing like my father. "You're okay," he said again, brushing my bangs away so I could see the sky. The stars had come out of nowhere, there were too many of them. Had they been there all night and I just hadn't noticed? "Who are you?" I finally asked, trying to sit up. He coaxed my shoulders to stay down. "That's not really important right now," he said, and he was right. It didn't matter who he was or who he wasn't. Or who they were or what they did and did not take from me. What mattered was that I could see the sky and that my body started to wake. I took a breath. I could feel every inch of me— pieces of glass stabbing my spine, cool bits of snow landing on the cuts on my lips—and I lay there, eyes wide open, naming every star as if I'd given birth to them centuries ago.

Club Orchid

Knowledge was dealing. Wink was winking. And I was in a club, sitting on a bench, listening to the Bee Gees for the third time in an hour with a laminated sign dangling from my neck.

Inside Club Orchid all the girls were chickens. On the slick vinyl bench, I sat with a lineup of black, brown, and white dance hostesses who squinted at their compact mirrors, painted their lips, teased and sprayed their bangs until they looked like trees against wind. They clucked their chewing gum and jerked their heads side to side, pointing at this and that and yakking and nudging their tails for more butt space on the bench. There was room next to me but I was new. They watched me without looking, stayed clear of me without effort. The next girl down on the bench was a country away, and I tried not to take the distance personally.

To the right of me, the cashier girl sat inside a clear, plastic cage and watched TV, the light twitching on her blank, paralyzed face. And to my left, a tall girl with spiky heels giggled her customer down a long hallway and into a private room. She was a pro. She knew the value of a leather miniskirt. I tried not to think about what went on in that room,

Out in front, about a hopscotch away, was the dance floor—a rectangular patch of shiny black linoleum with clusters of tiny tables around the perimeter. A disco ball spun over the center, smearing confetti on the mirrored walls, on the rising smoke, on the girls and their dates drinking and dancing and holding hands. Separating me from them was a gunky strip of carpet. It was green, like the bench. Jolly Rancher apple green. Olivia Newton-John sang over the speakers, and every girl had someone talking to them. I checked my armpits to make sure they didn't smell, patted my hair to calm the frizz, and adjusted the sign around my neck. From under my thigh I took out my book and started reading, trying to fool the universe into thinking I was fine alone.

I'd pulled *Gulliver's Travels* from a trash can. Half the

book, actually. Through the metal mesh, I could see the other half trapped under a folded pizza. There were too many people on the streets or else I might've reached in for it. Half a book and still it was thick. I kept my head down, read a sentence for the second time, and waited patiently for my number to be called. I didn't need anybody, I told myself, and read the sentence again.

But then Lana fell from the sky.

"Skanky freak," she said, and plunked down next to me. She was tall and black and had on a denim miniskirt that barely reached the tops of her long grasshopper legs. Right away I knew she wasn't a girl, not because of the way she looked but because she acted too much like one, too much drama in her hands and hips. Sitting inches from me, she folded her arms like a kid who'd lost a turn at something and crossed her legs tight, bouncing her foot to the beat of her anger. Even pissed off, she looked like an Egyptian princess. Her cheekbones sat high on her long, lean face, and her lashes, as thick as caterpillars, sparkled with silver dust. Lana fished a cigarette from her purse and tried to light it, but all of her trembled and the lighter kept getting lost in her giant, manicured hands. It took a few flicks before she was taking a drag so deep I thought I could feel air filling up in my own chest. I dog-eared my page and went over in my head all the things I could say to her:

Hey, the name's Joon, like the month but spelled like moon.

Sure, you can sit next to me, only if you give me a smoke.

Oh. I didn't know you were sitting next to me. Sure, we can talk. I can read later.

I slipped the book under my thigh. I'd never met a man dressed like a woman before and I wanted to make a good impression, I guess, prove to her that I was cool with her being different.

"Your cigarette smells like chocolate," was what finally came out of my mouth. I hadn't eaten that day and every smell was candy. She didn't hear me, though, and instead stayed focused on something out in front of us—on one of the tables on the dance floor.

"Aw, poor Lana," a girl said, about five heads down the bench. "You jealous cuz Marilyn's got a date?" The girl laughed and that cued the others to laugh, too, in that mean, high school sort of way.

"Listen, Miss Cocksucker," Lana pointed her cigarette at the girl. "If I was talking to you, you'd be hearing from my fist, okay?"

"Ooooo," all the girls sang, but Lana's gaze had already returned to the dance floor, where Bic the bartender weaved through a crowd and delivered a drink to a girl. The girl sat with two dates, even though she wasn't twice as pretty. And I guessed by her outfit that she was the one called Marilyn. She had platinum blond hair and wore a white halter-top dress, just like the one Marilyn Monroe had on when she stood over that subway grate. But besides that, the girl didn't look anything like Marilyn Monroe, nor did she have any of her manners. She sneered at Lana and gave her the finger, while mouthing *Fuck...you.*

"Fucking bitch!" Lana stood up and fireballed her purse, which completely missed the girl and instead smacked Bic on the back of his head as he was leaving the table. He took one look at Lana, picked up the purse by its gold chain, and hurled it back at her. Lana and I ducked. The purse ricocheted off the wall behind us and dropped to our feet. A lot of her makeup spilled out. The girls on the bench squealed and laughed and shouted things in Spanish. And the girl they called Marilyn chuckled with her hands and shoulders, as if to make up for the fact that we couldn't hear her, what with all the music. Then she went back to entertaining her two customers. One of them had on a white disco suit, even though it was already 1980.

A few people checked to see what all the fuss was about. The glittery lights slid over their dark faces as the excitement began to peter, and soon, it was as if the scene had never happened. Lana got down on her hands and knees to gather her things. I bent down to help her.

"Girls can be mean," I said, picking up a stray lipstick. "I used to get teased a lot, too."

She snatched the tube from my hand. "Who the fuck are you?"

I laughed a little without meaning to. "I'm number eight," I said, and pointed to the sign on my chest. Without a word, Lana went on clumping her things into both fists and jammed her purse under an armpit before getting up to leave. She was a monument, taller than anyone else in the club, maybe even Bic. When she walked away her arms flailed and her thigh-high skirt rocked side to side. I imagined walking the same way, doing the same with my hips and hands, until I noticed one of the girls on the bench staring at me.

I picked up the rest of Lana's things   a bus transfer, a packet of mayonnaise, a balled-up piece of paper. It was a handwritten receipt from the Plaza Motel, the same place where I was staying. She had paid thirty dollars for a night, twice as much as what I was paying. When I got up to throw everything away I noticed on the carpet a greasy black-and-white photo that looked to have been torn from a yearbook. It was of a boy with a perfect globe Afro, wearing a sweater and tie. An American flag waved in the background, and the name was scratched out in ink. The more I stared at him, the more I saw the likeness. The long cheekbones gave it away. He was maybe in the sixth grade or seventh, his eyes already bored with life. He didn't smile. He looked straight into the camera and maybe years beyond it.

I wondered when Lana had decided to start being a woman. If the change was easy or hard. If she had to forget people she loved and hated, and what piece of herself she had to leave behind. I wanted to start over, too. I'd left a bed and a mother to sleep under storefront awnings right beside men who thought a homeless girl was a warm radiator they could put their hands to. I'd slept in shelters, in abandoned buildings. I'd been beaten. And at the start of every new day, I still believed I could choose my own beginning, one that was scrubbed clean of everything past.

I shoved Lana's picture in my jeans pocket and sat

back down on the bench. I wanted to ask someone if they knew why Lana and Marilyn Monroe were fighting, but thought I'd better keep my trap shut. I fixed my sign and went back to my book. Part I, page thirty-eight. You gotta stay out of people's heads, I told myself.

The Bee Gees came on again, asking how deep my love was, and a customer got up, took his girl by the hand, and spun her to the middle of the dance floor. He danced like a stiff gorilla in his tight jeans and bomber jacket. She danced as if he wasn't there. I studied the customers— they were either fat and balding or skinny and short—their arms coiled around girls who wouldn't have given them a look outside this place. This wasn't a club. This was *Fantasy Island*, where for nine bucks an hour men were guaranteed to meet girls who liked them.

I didn't care about any of that, though. I was just glad to come in from the rain. After a long day of walking around looking for work at hot dog stands, pretzel carts, and grocery stores, it was nice to hear someone say, *You're hired,* just by looking at you. Like I was a model or something. Miss Mosely, the owner of the club, didn't require forms or IDs or ask how old I was or what school I had attended. She did ask, in that deep preacher voice of hers, if I was over eighteen. I didn't feel a drop of guilt

lying to her. I needed money. Jake, the manager at the
Plaza Motel, had said that since I couldn't find it in my
heart to sleep with him, I'd better come up with the
dough by midnight or else he'd give up my room. I looked
up at the clock above the front entrance. It read 9:30.
One night with my own ceiling above me, and I knew I
never wanted to sleep on the streets again. Every day I'd
have to make money, and every day my goal would have
to be one more motel night.

Jake charged fifteen bucks a day. The sheets were
an extra two, and I definitely needed the sheets to cover
up that bloodstain in the middle of the bed. The night
before, I had dreamed I was sleeping on a giant maxi pad,
and no matter how much I wiped the blood off my back,
new blood kept fizzing up from the mattress. In the morning, I couldn't get into the shower fast enough but then
jumped right back out when I saw the black slimy fungus
clinging to the tiles. I got a chill just looking at them, so
I decided not to. I put on my sneakers and stepped back
into the stall with my eyes shut, though it felt as if bugs
were crawling all around me. Even the water smelled. All
day I walked around with wet, spongy feet, but that was
okay since it rained anyway.

And it was still raining.

The front door of the club burst open and an Oriental man rushed in, brushing the rain off his shoulders with the brim of his fancy hat. He had guppy eyes, a wide moon face, and a basketball for a stomach. After scouring the place, he took off his trench coat, draped it over an arm, and walked up to the cashier window. All the girls on the bench snap-closed their compacts and sat up straight. You couldn't hear a single gum pop. I sat up, too, but only a little. I didn't want to act like a beauty-pageant contestant. A girl next to me smiled and blew him a kiss, which seemed like cheating. He smiled back at her as he plucked the fingers of his black leather gloves, one at a time. He watched us. I thought about smiling, too, except even the idea of it felt too desperate. I went back to reading, or at least I pretended to, and peeped at the man out the side of my pages. He paid in cash. I couldn't tell how much time he'd bought. The cashier, who was also Miss Mosely's daughter, cut off the music, and the speakers squawked before her voice shot through.

"Number eight!" she shouted, like a diner waitress. "*Número ocho!*"

The music came back on. I looked at my sign to double-check. Number eight. That was me. For a second, I felt I'd won something.

"That's bullshit," a girl said, standing up. She lit a cigarette and went on about how she didn't want no sorry-ass Chinaman anyhow. I got nervous. I didn't want one, either. Not a Chinaman. Not any man. I took off my sign, shoved that and my book behind the bench, and headed for the cashier's cage, slowly realizing with each step a few important things about me, like how I'd never been on a date, and never been a hostess of anything. I wasn't even a good dancer.

"His name's Eugene. Table twenty-three. Paid up for an hour," the cashier girl said. She was light-skinned, like Miss Mosely, half-black and half-white maybe, with small wrinkled ears that reminded me of walnuts. Mesmerized by the TV screen, she ate potato chips almost unknowingly. My mouth salivated at the thought of salt and vinegar. A commercial for Riunite came on, showing a woman toasting her glass, which was decorated with a cherry and a juicy-looking orange.

A plasticized map showing the layout of the club was taped to the counter. Table twenty-three sat in the back corner of the dance floor.

"Don't forget to punch in," the girl said, pointing down, her eyes never leaving the TV screen.

I said thanks, checked below the counter, pulled my

card out from the rack and fed the clock, which gave it a stamp of 10:02.

I headed toward the back of the club, walked down the green carpeting, down the length of the bar, where Bic sat next to the cash register, his eyes married to a paper. A slow song came on... *She's out of my life*... and some couples got up and danced, their necks hooked as one. Other girls stayed seated, looking like trophies next to their dates. I got a better look at the girl in the Marilyn Monroe dress. She sat with her arms around both her guys, leaning in close to one, and then the other, as if playing telephone. Then she stood up, fixed her breasts, and led her men down the long hallway where the light was thick and yellow.

Watching all this was Lana. She stood at the bar, smoking, her eyes fixed on Marilyn. I reached into my back pocket, only to decide that maybe now wasn't the right time to give back the picture. So I kept walking, pointing my chin straight ahead, trying not to look at Lana, which was like trying not to scratch an itch on your nose.

"You following me?" she asked as I passed her.

"What? No." I pointed to my guy. He was dabbing the bald spot on his head with a napkin.

"Maybe he's got a friend for me," she said, smoothing down her hair. "I wanna look good for his friend. How'm I looking right now?"

She looked drunk. And bitter. Her eyes were as shiny as her lip gloss, and her voice had fallen about an octave. She sounded like a truck.

"You look good," I said.

"Well, isn't that sweet." She took a swig of her drink. Like a broken doll, when she tipped her head back her eyelids came down, and then stayed down. "Hey, where you going? I'm still talking to you."

I hadn't moved. "I'm right here," I told her.

She squeezed one eye, forcing the other to open. "I'm sorry about, you know..." Her drink pointed out the bench area. "This your first night?"

I nodded.

"Well, I'd say congratulations but this place is hell, so you're fucked." She put her glass down and tried to light a cigarette but the flame refused to meet the tip.

"I should probably get going." My customer was now taking off his wristwatch and setting it on the table.

Lana finally lit her cigarette and took a drag. "Well, I hope you and your father have a very nice time."

I was about to correct her but then got the joke. I turned to leave.

"Guess you think I'm a freak, huh?" she asked.

I turned back and told her that I didn't, that I'd liked her from the moment I saw her.

"Oh yeah? Why's that?" She faced the dark dance floor, and, as drunk as she was, she was waiting for my answer.

"I don't know. Maybe because you don't remind me of anyone."

"Mmm…" Lana smiled and a gauze of smoke slithered from her lips. "I like that," she said. "You're good. You'll do just fine." She about-faced and walked the length of the bar, using the stools as a guide. "Come find me later. We'll get you some makeup."

"Okay," I shouted. "That sounds really, really…" I told myself to stop smiling and nodding because by that point, I was alone. But I didn't feel alone. As I headed toward my date, I replayed the conversation with Lana in my mind until all the awkwardness fell from my words and I sounded as cool as an old-time movie star.

I made it to the table.

"Is anyone sitting here?" I asked, my voice now tinged

with confidence. As Miss Mosely had instructed, I smiled as big as I could with my lips and eyes.

"I'm sorry. Did you say something?" he said, pretending he hadn't heard me. By the way he folded his hands on the table, I could tell he wanted me to say it again, once more, with feeling.

"Can I sit here?" I asked, testing out a sultry voice.

He gestured big at the chair across. "Yes, of course."

I sat down.

Behind him, over his shoulder, I could see Lana standing at the far end of the bar, leaning her chest and body against the counter, one leg vining the other. She was talking to Bic, who crossed his arms and shook his head. Then he handed her something from his pocket, which Lana took and popped into her mouth.

My date stirred his drink with the plastic sword, one way, and then the other, without looking up. The light from the disco ball skated round and round his balding head and a full minute went by, and not a word. Except for a few sighs here and there. Maybe he didn't like the way I looked up close. Maybe he'd picked me because I was the only Oriental and he felt sorry for me. I was definitely the worst-dressed girl there—had on jeans and sneakers when all the others wore skirts that gave men something to look at. And I was the only one without makeup. I checked my nails and saw that they were clean, which made me feel a little better. *Say something nice about his clothes*—Miss Mosely had told me this would get things rolling, but what could I say about a white button-down shirt?

"Look. I don't know why I'm here." His voice startled me. "I suppose I'm a little lonely, I don't have many friends, and, well, let's face it, I won't be winning any awards for the 'best-looking guy' category." He said all this really fast, like a pull-toy running out of string. I hadn't expected him to be this way.

"You look okay." I noticed that his shirt was new, the creases making the letter H on his chest. I pictured him at the store, buying this shirt just for tonight. "Better than okay," I added. "I really like the buttons on your shirt."

"Thanks. That's kind of you to say." He touched a button, and then, without warning, put both of his hands on mine, squeezing too tightly.

Bic came by. "Another whiskey?" he asked my date. I took my hand back.

"Do you have to sneak up on us like that?" the man said, louder than I thought he should.

"I'm six foot three. If you can't see me coming, that's

your problem." Bic put a napkin down in front of me. "What do you want?"

"I'm fine," I said, but Bic didn't leave. "I'm not that thirsty."

"You sure," he said, not asking, but telling. Bic stood wider than a door, with an L-shaped jaw and an angry crew cut.

"Riunite on ice?" I said.

"What?" Bic squeezed his eyes. "We don't got that."

Then I remembered Miss Mosely telling me to order vodka so Bic could serve me water and it would look the same.

"Vodka?" I asked.

"Excellent choice," he said, and walked off.

"With two cherries," I yelled after him. "And an orange!" I was starving.

"Do you think he heard me?" I asked my date, who was now wiping his face up and down with both hands, as if he were washing it. Then he rattled his head to shake off the invisible water, took a deep breath, held it, and let it out, sending me a wave of garlic. Just as I thought he was finished, he made big clownish smiles that looked more painful than cheery, before scooting his chair closer to the table. He sat upright and tall. He was a new man, and he was going to take it from the top.

"Hi, my name's Eugene." He put his hand out for a shake. "What's yours?"

I shook it. "Joon-Mee."

"Joon-Mee. Now, there's a name you don't hear every day."

"Actually, I pretty much hear it every day," I said.

He didn't laugh. "Where do you work?" he asked, and he wasn't kidding.

I leaned in. "Are you okay?"

He blinked, something like five times in a row, and took a mechanical sip of his drink before megaphoning his hands over his mouth. "WHERE DO YOU WORK?"

"Uh, I work—"

"What college do you attend?"

"Sure. I mean. Yes." I couldn't keep up.

"You must get good grades. I always did," he said, slinging an arm over the back of his chair. "You look like you'd be good in school."

"Yup." I nodded. "I got A's in everything."

"Everything?" He smirked and took a drink.

"I might be flunking gym."

"I didn't know they had gym in college."

Whatever game he had in his head, I didn't want to play anymore. My mouth was dirt dry. I sat silent while he stared into me long and watched me twist my napkin into worms.

I was glad Bic came back when he did. He put my drink down (no cherry, no orange) and Eugene said, "No, no, I've got it," although I hadn't offered to pay. He pulled out a fistful of money, flashed a smile, and counted slowly. They were mostly ones. He handed Bic a few bills and told him to keep the rest.

"Great, I can make that phone call now," he said.

Eugene's face turned stiff to Bic's sarcasm. As soon as Bic was gone, I took huge gulps of the water—it felt good to wet my throat—and stopped only when Eugene gave me a puzzled look. I remembered the water was supposed to be vodka, and made that face actors make after downing a stinging shot of alcohol.

"In any case, don't you want to know what *I* do for a living?" Eugene asked.

"Mmm . . . sure."

"I just thought a girl in your situation might want to hear about other people's career choices."

"I said *okay*."

He tensed his jaws, the hinges bulging as he ground his teeth. Right. He wanted to be asked.

"What do you do for a living?" I sat up, tucked my hands under my thighs. I couldn't decide if I should be scared of him.

"Let's just say I have a job most people don't realize how tough it is. Would you like to guess?"

"Are you a cop?" Miss Mosely said that cops got everything half-off, unless they were planning to raid the place, in which case they got everything on the house.

"Me? No... but I could've been NYPD, I suppose. I'm in good shape for my age. Okay. Keep going."

"A baker."

He didn't like this guess much. "Go on," he said, his voice low.

"A math teacher."

He showed his annoyance by loudly sucking air through his nose and exhaling silently through O-shaped lips.

"Are you a doctor?"

Now his mouth stretched into a crooked smile. He nodded. "That's a very good guess. My sister's a surgeon, so I guess I could've been one, too." His eyes traveled to a faraway land. "But I wanted more freedom in my life," he said, shrugging. "What can I say? I didn't want a pager telling me what to do."

That was when I looked past Eugene, over his shoulder, and saw Marilyn Monroe walking out from the back hallway with her two dates in tow, the guy in the white disco suit checking his zipper. Marilyn escorted him and his buddy across the front of the club, passing the bench of girls and the cashier stand, and showed them to the door. After blowing several kisses at them and waving goodbye, she turned and beamed at Lana, who still stood by the bar. Marilyn walked up to her and whispered something into Lana's ear, before stepping onto the dance floor, where her new date holding flowers waited at a table. Lana could've set her on fire the way she was staring.

"Okay. Give up?" Eugene asked.

"Yeah," I said, and watched Lana slam down her glass and zigzag onto the dance floor. She crashed into a table, knocked over a chair, and then another, which made her keel over onto the table where Marilyn sat arm-in-arm with her date. Without missing a beat, Lana threw up all over Marilyn.

"I work with diamonds. Wouldn't have guessed it, right?"

Marilyn shrieked and jumped from her seat, cursing and fanning her hands over her huge breasts, now slick with vomit.

"Hell-o? Anyone home?" Eugene snapped his fingers at my face.

I flashed back to him. "That must be exciting. Touching diamonds every day."

"Well, not diamonds, exactly. Cubic zirconium. CZs we call them. They're just like the real deal. They're actually heavier than diamonds and can cut glass, which isn't too difficult, as glass is only six-point-five on the hardness scale and..."

I looked behind him again. Marilyn shouted, "Fuck you!" or something like that to Lana, and Lana bent down, grabbed Marilyn's date by the ears and kissed him, and stayed kissed, as if it were a breath-holding contest. The date, a small wrinkle of a man, tried to push her off and Marilyn slapped Lana on the back of her head, but Lana couldn't be moved. She kept kissing and didn't come up for air.

"...and sometimes I can guess their weight with only a glance. It's a terrific workout for the mind. All my employees, they can't believe how close I can estimate."

Lana finally unglued her face from the date's, and as

soon as he was free, he coughed and spat bullets on the floor. He seemed more stunned than angry as he yanked his jacket and ran toward the front entrance, wiping his mouth on his sleeve. Then Lana really did something I hadn't expected. She reached for Marilyn's face and tried to kiss her. Marilyn wasn't having any of it, though. She screamed something, either *I don't owe you* or *I don't know you*, and pushed Lana to the floor before marching off. Slumped on the floor like that, Lana looked lost. She screamed up at the disco ball, told it to shut the fuck up, but the ball kept spinning and the music kept playing, whereas the people in the club stood frozen. Everyone seemed to be looking at her. Everyone except Eugene.

"...especially my sister. She thinks she's pretty special for being a surgeon. What she doesn't understand is that she owes it all to me. I took over the family's business, so she could do whatever she wanted, and she's never once thanked..."

Miss Mosely marched out from her office with Marilyn the tattletale following close. Lana was going to get in trouble.

I stood up. "I have to use the bathroom."

"What?" Eugene grabbed my arm. His strength surprised me.

"I have to go," I said, and pulled free.

The flashing lights made it hard to focus but you couldn't miss Miss Mosely. She had a pin head and a thick torso—a drumstick squeezed into a ruby-red sequined dress that played miniskirt in front, evening gown in back. The dress tongued the floor behind her as she walked up to Lana, pinched the back of her arm, and ushered her off the dance floor and toward the back hallway. I followed at a distance, and when the three of them stopped in the middle of the hallway, I slid into the bathroom, left the door ajar, and peeked from there.

"Now, what was so damn important I had to hang up on my husband?"

"*Pendeja's* psycho, that's what's going on," Marilyn yelled. She puckered her lips and waved her finger, making Zs in the air. This was the first time I'd seen her up close, and I hadn't noticed that underneath all that wig, she was very Dominican.

"At least I ain't a lying bitch slut," Lana said, trying her best to stay standing.

"*Ay, puta borracha*. Listen, *maricón*, when we're working I ain't your friend or whatever the fuck you think I am, okay? I got kids, okay? So you better not fuck with me making money, or I swear I'll—"

Lana spit at Marilyn, and soon their fists and heads got tangled up in a big, ugly bow. Lana clutched a handful of Marilyn's hair but all she got was the wig, and Marilyn screamed and dug her nails across Lana's face, scratching her up good. It was strange watching a fight that wasn't being stopped by anyone. In school, a teacher always wedged in, and that was that, but Miss Mosely simply stepped aside and raised a chubby finger for Bic to come over.

Even before Bic arrived, Lana and Marilyn grew tired and quit fighting on their own. Marilyn snatched her wig out of Lana's hands, and Lana, she didn't look too good. The fight had taken the bones out of her. She slacked against the wall and slid down until her butt reached carpet. Her lipstick was smeared, and her long, skinny legs were spread out in a V, showing a black lacy bulge of underwear.

"Clean this mess up," Miss Mosely said to Bic when he got there. "And you." She turned to Marilyn, who was in the middle of slipping her wig back on. "I want nothing more from you the rest of the night. You *comprende* what I'm saying?"

That's when Miss Mosely caught me peeking, which shocked me enough to shut the bathroom door and run into a stall. Minutes later, when I realized she wasn't coming after me, I poked my head out into the hallway again. Only Bic and Lana were there.

"Rise and shine." Bic nudged Lana's thigh with the tip of his cowboy boot. Lana was out. One of her fake eyelashes had fallen off, which made it seem like she was forever winking. Bic pulled her up by the wrists and slung her onto his back, like a knapsack, and lugged her down the hallway, not caring that her shoes had slipped off. Her nylon toes dragged along the carpet.

I looked both ways before coming out of the bathroom. I gathered up Lana's shoes and tiptoed down the hall to where Bic had taken her. There were two doors—one marked TV ROOM, the other, EXIT. I opened that one, but Bic beat me to it and came back in, alone.

"Where do you think you're going?"

"I was just—" I held up the shoes in my defense.

"If I were you, I'd get my ass back to work." He pushed me down the hall, and I tripped and fell. My nose hit the carpet, and I dropped the shoes. Before I could think about collecting them, Bic's cement hands locked onto the side of my arms and hoisted me up.

"Don't." I squirmed to get away.

"Yeah, yeah," he said, and moved me along. I tried

to twist my arms free, to kick him in the legs, to elbow him. I fought with every part of me but he wouldn't give. I felt dizzy. My nose burned. I kicked his shins and hit his chest with the back of my head but it was clear I was just hurting myself.

He shoved me off. "Fine. I don't have time for your shit anyway."

I ran back into the bathroom and shut the door, leaned against it to catch my breath.

"Hey, Chinita!"

Marilyn stood in front of the mirror, the top of her dress peeled down to her waist. She was bent over, with her huge jelly breasts dangling above the sink, rubbing pink soap crystals onto her chest. Her back was bare, syrupy skin, and she had on black high heels with long vinyl straps that drew Xs up her calves. I walked up to the sink and looked down. Ladybug drops of blood fell, one by one, onto the metal basin.

"Ay, *puta*, your nose is bleeding," she said.

"Yeah. I guess it is."

"Don't worry, Chinita, it gets better. I promise." The spikes of her heels scraped the bathroom tile as she ran into a stall and grabbed a wad of toilet paper. "The first day's the hardest. That's cuz you got all that crap in your brains about right and wrong and shit. That shit can kill you."

I clamped my nose with tissue and tilted my head back. I told her that I didn't understand.

"That's what I'm esplaining." Marilyn rinsed her breasts and made sure not to let any water drizzle down her dress. "Me? I'm a successful businesswoman cuz I don't care about nothing but working and working hard. That's it. Been hostessing for five years and it's a good living. My two girls, they get skating lessons, dancing lessons, whatever they want, cuz on a good night, I'm on the clock, like all the time, okay? Fifteen cents a minute, times whatever, plus some of them like to pay a little extra, for, you know, the TV room and shit. Add that up and that's a Benjamin. Easy. Take away what I gotta give Miss Mosely, but after that, that's all *my* money. Stick with this and you can bank, okay?"

Marilyn finished washing. I wondered if Miss Mosely made her say this to all the new girls.

"But not everybody got the cash for something extra. Some of 'em just wanna sit there and blah-blah-blah." She yanked on the cloth towel machine, two clicks, and dabbed her chest. "Why make five bucks hearing some guy complaining about the job thing or the wife thing, when you can charge twenty bucks for a five-minute massage, you know?"

"I think so."

On the mirror in front of me, someone had drawn a picture of a bird flying over an ocean of curlicue waves, except that the bird looked more like a football with wings. And below that, a girl with a penis drilled through her mouth and out the back of her head.

"How old are your kids?" I asked, suddenly exhausted. I leaned against the wall.

"Seven and nine. You wanna see?"

From her purse she pulled out a wallet and flipped it open to a studio photo.

"The older one's got pretty eyes," I said.

"She wants to be a lawyer when she grows up. I tell her, why you want that? Sit behind a desk all day. You could be an artist or a poetess, and write poetry. That's what I would do. I like writing about lovebirds and shit like that. I got a poem published in the *National Enquirer.* It's called 'Love Birds.' It's about love. Don't worry, Chinita, I read it for you sometime, okay?" She pulled her dress back up, made sure she was good, reached into her purse again and this time pulled out a little vial. She popped it open. "I gotta get back out there, but listen, I'm gonna give you some avice, okay? One." She swallowed two pills—one white, one pink. "Take a lotta drugs. Nah, I'm just fucking with you. But not really." She picked out a cigarette and lit up. "Okay. One." She held her cigarette way above her head, keeping the smoke from reaching her. "This avice is very important, so listen careful. Don't ever, I mean ever, steal any a my dates." She looked in the mirror and tugged on a few strands of her wig. "And two. Sometimes you gotta sacrifice to get what you really want, okay? That's the truth. And three . . ." She shouldered the strap of her purse. "When your date esplodes in your mouth, don't pull out."

I turned on the faucet. I couldn't look at her. "That's some advice," I said.

"You gotta keep it there and take it all in. You do that and you got a date for life, Chinita. For life."

Marilyn opened the door to leave, and the sounds of the club swam in and out. I rinsed my face. The water felt good. I patted my face dry with a wad of toilet paper, and with each dab, I felt myself returning to normal. And the more normal I felt, the more I had to make sure Lana was all right. I felt I understood her. Her trying to make do with who she was now. I hoped Bic hadn't thrown her out. I wondered where she was and if she knew that her feet were bare. Maybe he'd put her in one of the private rooms. Maybe even a brick like him understood that a person shouldn't be on the streets without shoes.

When I stepped out into the hallway, the blaring music crushed whatever exhaustion I felt. The clock above the entrance read 11:00. I still had time. So far I'd been clocked in for an hour, which meant nine bucks. I needed seventeen for the room and sheets, nineteen if I wanted to grab a cheese slice. The bench was almost empty and the dance floor was busy with bodies making promises. I didn't think Lana would be out there but I looked for her in the crowd anyway, just in case.

That's when I saw Eugene, at our table, talking to Miss Mosely.

"...then she just vanished," he said as I ran up. "If I wanted bullshit, I would've stayed at home with my wife."

"Just calm down, Eugene."

"Don't tell me what to do," he shot back. "I paid in advance."

"Yes, you're a good customer, and if you let me finish, I guarantee you, you're going to be very happy."

"I was planning to bring all my buddies here next week," he said.

"You don't have any friends, remember?" I said, angry and hurt that he had told on me.

Miss Mosely touched my shoulder. "We listen with our lips shut, okay?"

"Do you see how rude she is? I want a refund."

"As I was saying . . . half an hour in the TV room, with any girl you want, on the house."

He clenched his jaws and considered this. "Nope. It's too late. You've ruined it by talking about it."

"Now, we went over this before, Eugene. We can't fix the problem if we can't discuss it."

"But I don't like discussing it. I come here so I don't have to discuss it. I come here so that everything's easy. Do you know how hard I work all day?"

"Here we go," I mumbled.

"One more word"—Miss Mosely placed a hand on my face—"and I never see you again, you hear me?" Her hand then moved from my face to Eugene's chest, smoothing down a crease on his shirt. "Now. Are we taking the room or not?"

The red seemed to have drained from his cheeks. I wanted to slap it back in. "Two free drinks," he said.

"Done."

"And any girl I want."

"Completely up to you."

That was the best thing I'd heard all night. I even thought to recommend Marilyn to him, but he was busy now, scanning the entire club slowly, raising and dropping his brows at the thought of every girl—no, no, maybe, no, no—until he got to me.

"This one," he said, pointing me out with his chin.

"What? Why?"

"It is a strange choice, I have to admit," Miss Mosely said.

Eugene grabbed his coat by the back of its neck and tossed it over his arm. "I think there's a lesson to be learned here," he said, and tucked his gloves into his hat, pinching the brim shut.

"Suit yourself." Miss Mosely took my elbow and gave me a look that said everything.

"I don't want to," I whispered to her.

"Now, be a good hostess. You do this and I'll give you a Friday night shift, okay?"

"But I really don't want—"

"Mr. Otaki's been a regular for years now, so take good care of him." She hooked my arm around his and soon Eugene and I were walking arm-in-arm across the dance floor and down the long yellow hallway with Miss

Mosely right behind us holding our elbows in place and reminding us in that deep preacher voice of hers how everything was going to be just fine.

"Don't forget my drinks," he said, over his shoulder.

"Not a chance," she said, and unlocked the door.

The TV room smelled like fish and Lysol. As soon as we went in, he bolted the door and flipped a switch that turned on a bulb overhead. It was a red light, the kind that made you think your eyes were on fire. On the end table, next to the couch, was a bag of white cotton balls and, next to that, two large plastic bottles. Both had masking tape on the front—one labeled OIL, the other ALCOHOL, in black marker. His face was more raisin in this light. Even my own hands looked old and wrinkled. He walked over to the TV, turned it on, and sat on the couch. The reception was sandy but clear enough for me to see Chuck Scarborough finish the news and wish me goodnight. Eugene had already unbuckled his pants. He leaned back and looked up at the ceiling with his eyes shut tight, like he was praying for something specific.

"What are you doing?" he asked, opening one eye.

I wasn't doing anything.

"Grab that bottle and wash me off." And just like that, he pulled it out from his pants. No game. No playacting.

His penis hung from his zipper like a shriveled tongue. It had too much skin. Chicken skin. I didn't want to be in the same room with it, let alone touch it.

"Is this something I need to talk to your boss about?"

I told him no and grabbed the alcohol bottle, the cotton, and got on the floor. The crusty carpet bit my knees as I held his penis with the tip of my index finger and swabbed it with cotton.

"What the hell's wrong with you?" He knocked the cotton out of my hand. "Just stop acting like you don't know what to do. You know everything, right? You're a smart-ass. Just because you're a pretty girl you think you don't have to do anything you don't want to. You think you're too good for this, right?"

"No."

"You think you're better than everybody, sitting there, reading your stupid book. You're not. You're gonna have to get dirty just like the rest us," he said, and shoved my head down between his legs. The alcohol stung my eyes. I couldn't breathe, and the smell of him choked me. He held me down by the neck and used his free hand to wedge his penis into my mouth. My eyes swelled, something warm slid from my nose, and no matter how much I pushed to get away, I couldn't. The harder I hit him, the harder he pushed down, and not long after that, I gave in. It seemed logical. To get him off as fast as I could. To give whatever it was he wanted me to give. He let out a cry. He pinched my ear, twisted it, stuck a finger inside it and cried some more, and a couple of times he whispered his own name, until finally, he let out a long wail and slackened his grip. I turned my head and spit. I coughed and spat and coughed again but all I could taste was sourness. Bitter milk. Spoiled fungus rice.

He fell asleep almost instantly. Asleep with his penis still out. I stood over him and watched him for a while—his chest rising and dipping, the hair sprouting from his ears, the cluster of acne under his chin. I hated him. I couldn't believe that earlier I'd worried about him not liking me. That seemed like years ago. I held the bottle of oil in my hand but I didn't know how it had gotten there. Or how I'd gotten there. I tried to retrace my steps, to think of all the things that had happened to put me in that red room, but the only thing that kept coming to mind was the taste of him. I bent down, pinched his nose, and jammed the bottle of oil into his mouth. I gave it a hard squeeze and ran.

Down the hallway, through the dance floor. I felt a rush traveling through me—that nervous thrill you get when you fly in your dreams. I cut through couples, ran up to the bench, grabbed my book, and headed for the cashier. I pulled out my timecard and punched it in. I was all right. It was eleven-thirty.

"I want to get paid for tonight," I said to the cashier girl who was in the middle of blowing a strawberry bubble and watching *The Odd Couple*. I couldn't stop shaking. I looked back at the hallway. Eugene was stumbling out of the room, one hand on the doorjamb, the other clutching his throat.

"Hey!" I slammed the counter. "I want to cash out."

"Just wait your fucking turn," the girl said.

I looked behind me. "There's no one else here."

"Yeah, yeah." She finally got off her chair and read my timecard. "What's your number?"

Eight, I told her, eight, and with that she clacked the keys on her calculator. I checked for Eugene again and found him standing in the middle of the dance floor, under the disco ball, looking right at me.

"Shit, I did that wrong," the girl said. "Okay. Fifteen cents a minute is nine dollars an hour, and you worked an hour and a half, so that makes . . . Wait, what is it?" she asked the calculator.

"Thirteen-fifty, and plus..." I didn't know how to say it. "I was in the room."

"That you get from the date," she said. "We only rent you the space."

Eugene was now snaking through the dance floor, with Miss Mosely by his side.

"O-kay." The cashier girl counted the bills onto the counter, one dollar at a time, slower than anyone dead. "Take away what you owe for the room..." She studied the calculator again. That's when I slid the money into my book and bolted.

I ran so hard so fast. Cars and lights streaked by me. Gated storefronts. Pieces of cardboard covering bodies and dogs. The rain hadn't let up. I turned around. Bic shot out the front door and I bumped head-on into a couple holding hands. I didn't stop and I didn't apologize. A bus sped by and I ran faster, across the street, turned a corner, and then another, and it wasn't until I was a few blocks away that I could muster the courage to look back again. There was no one behind me, and my legs started to slow. Bic's not there, I told myself over and over while trying to catch my breath. I kept walking. The streets were empty, except for a few strands of people far ahead. It was okay. No one was after me. At the first chance I could, I leaned over a trash can and stuck a finger down my throat.

I got to the Plaza Motel before midnight. I was cold and wet but I walked slowly anyway and looked up at the rain, how it fell so pretty on the pink neon sign that read NO VACANCY. Hiding from the weather, people slept under the bus stop shelter that stood in front of the motel entrance. Some wore ponchos made of black garbage bags and others clutched their blankets of flattened boxes. FRAGILE. HANDLE WITH CARE, one said, and I couldn't tell if I wanted to laugh or cry. There was only one bench, and a woman took up all of it, slept on it sideways with her long legs slightly bent. I guess I knew it was Lana before I went up to her. Her feet were bare, her lips were bruised, and she looked to have marbles jammed in her left cheek. I shook her awake.

"Leave me alone," she said, pushing me away.

The motel lobby smelled sour. Jake sat in his cage, a glass booth surrounded by a grid of metal bars. He talked on the phone while shoveling sauerkraut from a jar straight into his mouth. I sat Lana down on a step near the elevator. She was still half asleep and kept drooping to one side. I let the wall catch her. I wasn't sure if she even remembered who I was. My guess was that she would've gone along with anyone that night.

"I'll call you back," Jake said as I stepped up to the window.

"I made it." I pulled out the thirteen-fifty from my book and pushed it through the cage's small opening. I apologized for the money being a little soggy, and for being a buck-fifty short. "I'll get you the rest tomorrow," I promised.

He gave me a flat smile and glanced over at Lana. "What's that?" he asked, pointing with his fork.

"She's my friend."

"Oh yeah? That's too bad because I just kicked your friend out. She still owes me from last week." His tiny jaws didn't have enough room for all his teeth. They crawled on top of one another.

"She's staying with me, just for one night," I said, trying to sound casual.

Jake took another forkful of sauerkraut and talked while something clear leaked from the corners of his lips. "It's another ten for a guest."

"But I don't have another ten."

"That's the rules."

"But it's already midnight, and she's just gonna sleep."

He picked his front teeth with his tongue and made a sucking sound.

"Look," I whispered into the window. "It's been kind of a rough night." I cleared my throat. I didn't want to cry, not in front of him. "I'm really trying to make things okay. If you let me and my friend in, then all of it was worth it. Do you understand?"

He pointed his fork skyward. "Rules are rules."

The motel policy sign above the cage had a lot of words on it, words that meant nothing. I wanted to climb up and tear the sign down. I wanted to punch my hand through the glass, let the jagged pieces slice into my arm as I grabbed Jake by the throat and made him understand. "Don't you get it? Everything would be fine if you'd just stop being a fucking dick."

It wasn't easy walking with Lana. She was still half asleep or high, I couldn't tell, but we made it to a bus stop two blocks from the motel. We sat on the bench. I told her to lean against me but that didn't work because she was too tall. So she lay on her side, with her head on my lap. I told her that everything was good. I figured we could ride around for a while, which would be warmer than sleeping outside. I asked her if she had any money. She didn't answer. Jake had refused to give back my thirteen-fifty. He called it a nonrefundable deposit. I threatened to call the cops. He told me to go ahead, knowing I wouldn't. He folded my cash and shoved it in his shirt pocket. I checked Lana's pockets; all I could find were two pills. They looked so black in my palm, and then they looked like food. I didn't think too long. I swallowed them both and watched Lana breathe.

"Who did this to you?" I asked. Her face seemed worse than it had at the club.

"What?" she mumbled.

"Who beat you up?"

She tongued the blister on her bottom lip as if to confirm what I'd just said. "Nobody. Me. Everybody," she said, without opening her eyes.

Cars slushed by. The rain stopped, making the road look vinyl. Down a ways, a row of traffic lights blinked red and yellow, and even farther down, a street-cleaning

truck turned the corner. The sidewalks were empty.
There was no one—no one to bother us. Lana was out
again. Her head felt heavy on my lap, and soon I couldn't
feel my legs. Maybe Marilyn was right. In order to get
what I needed—shelter, food, money, friendship—parts
of me, piece by piece, would have to be sacrificed. From
my back pocket I pulled out the yearbook photo and held
it to Lana's face for comparison. As a boy she looked thin
and breakable. I understood then what I had admired
about her. Over her old self, she had grown a new crust,
a new version that didn't remind anyone, maybe not even
her, of anything past.

I looked down the street for any hints of a bus. The
storefront windows were dark, and the sky, a beautiful
empty. Everything was closed. Everything was black,
except for the 99-cent store across the street. The light
inside was so bright, you thought you were looking into
the sun. All the aisles were bleach-white, the floors wet
and sparkly, and the huge window, the size of two movie
screens, was lined with orange, blue, pink, yellow, and
red containers of soap. Bottles and boxes of all kinds
of detergents—dishwasher, laundry, kitchen floor, you
name it, they were all there, like an open box of crayons.
Every aisle was clean and every shelf was crammed full

with merchandise, and you knew nothing was ever kept in storage, absolutely nothing, no extra supply, no secret shipments hiding in the back. Everything the store had to offer was all right there, completely exposed, and I was happy to be seeing it all.

Knowledge

We were sitting on a bench in Union Square, waiting for Duffy the dealer to show up with a new batch of speed-balls. Knowledge leaned back and stretched her legs out, and I did, too, letting the afternoon light seep through our jeans and T-shirts.

"You keeping good these days?" she asked.

I told her I was.

"Where're you shacked up?"

I told her I was fine.

"I didn't ask *how* you were, I asked where are you staying."

"The ferry," I said. "Sometimes the subway."

She nodded. "The ferry's nice. You can't beat the view."

"One of these days I'm going to go to Ellis Island and see the Statue of Liberty up close," I said.

She cringed with disgust. "Why you have to go and say that?"

"Say what?"

"We're sitting here, having a nice conversation, and all of a sudden you say cheesy shit like wanting to see the Statue of Liberty. And anyway, it's not on Ellis."

It hurt me when she criticized. On the streets she was my teacher, my mother, and I wanted her approval as much as I wanted money.

"You don't need to see the Statue of Liberty to know you're free."

"I didn't say that."

"That shit's for tourists. Like her."

A woman sat down on the bench across from us, her fingers, as plump as larvae, gripping a purse to her chest. "You're free right now," Knowledge continued. "You can do whatever you want with your life." A few pigeons landed near us and began pecking by our feet. "You think I'm gonna be dealing for the rest of my life? You think I'm working like this so I can live under a bridge? Fuck that."

Knowledge had thick shoulders, a boxer's nose, and a pointed chin that shot out from her neck like a spade ready to dig. She was the hardest-working pusher I knew and maybe the only one who never used. "The harder you work, the luckier you get," she said, showing me the underside of her arm where she had inked the very words.

"Is that tattooed?"

She looked like she might hit me. "You turn stupid since I saw you last?"

"Why're you yelling?"

She licked an index finger and rubbed a letter off. "Don't you ever get a tattoo, understand? All it says is that you ain't open to change."

"You don't have to be so mad."

"Yes I do," she said, locking eyes with me. "Least until you grow up."

"I'm grown."

"Well..." she said with a smirk. "You still got more learning to do." She laced her hands behind her head and smiled at the trees and the sky. "But that's okay. That's what I'm here for."

"Yeah. That's what you're here for," I said.

The sun loved us that afternoon. It loved the birds and the grass and the benches all equally. I looked at the woman across from us. The sun was loving her a little too much. Her face was red, as if her too-tight sweater was pushing all the blood in her body up to her two bulbous cheeks. A pair of pink spandex leggings encased the rest of her, showing every pockmark on her thighs.

"Damn, I wish I had a pool," Knowledge said, tilting her chin closer to the sun.

A pair of pigeons waddled over to the woman, and she cooed and smiled at them too loudly, as if she were onstage.

"Bet you guys would like a snack, is that what you want?" she asked the birds. Then she yelled across to us: "These pigeons are everywhere!"

Knowledge leaned in and whispered, "You see the way she talks to us? She's one of them types that likes to think she's cool enough to talk to us poor little people."

"It's such a gorgeous day, isn't it?" she asked us.

"Maybe she's just being nice," I whispered.

"Go ahead. Answer the bitch, you think she's so nice." Knowledge smacked my shoulder and looked away.

"Yeah, it's pretty sunny," I said to the woman. "Are you from out of town?"

"I said answer her. I didn't say nothing about asking her questions."

"From Savannah. Georgia. Do you know where that is?"

"Aw shit, she's from the south. She think she's gotta be nice to the slaves."

"Kind of. I've never been there, though."

"Okay, you can stop talking to her now."

"Boy, these birds are really aggressive," the woman said, and from her bag, she produced a hairbrush, a subway map, and a wallet and laid them on the bench beside her before fishing out a bag of Pepperidge Farm cookies. With a look of romance in her eyes she crumbled the cookies and tossed them to the ground, and none of us noticed the man walk up to her.

"My wallet!" the woman screamed suddenly, pointing at the thief, who was now speeding through the square. And not a second later, Knowledge took off after him.

"He's got my wallet!" the woman said again, just to me, and I could tell she was still a few minutes away from actually believing that her wallet was gone. I was already a block behind but I ran after Knowledge anyway.

Years after this, but long before she was shot and left to bleed to death across the street from Bronx-Lebanon Hospital, Knowledge found herself standing in line at a downtown bank, her clammy hands holding a stickup note. She would tell me that her heart pounded slower but worked harder, trying to pump out what felt like oatmeal instead of blood. As her body inched along the velvet rope, she prayed for things, like a small fire, a power outage, even another bank robbery. Anything to stop her from committing the felony her boyfriend had sent her on. Time moved both fast and slow, and neither speed synced up with her fears as she stood at the head of the line. The tellers looked too chipper for a Monday morning. Did they even have money on Mondays? she wondered. Shouldn't she have come on a Friday? She couldn't remember why she opened the stickup note, just that she did, and that her boyfriend, the first and only boy she'd ever dated, was the one who had penned it: *This is a stickup. Give me all your monie.*

The misspelling stopped her.

"Next in line," a teller called.

Knowledge herself had quit school in the ninth grade but she couldn't believe that he had misspelled money. "What kind of an idiot can't spell money?" she told me. "How fucking stupid do you have to be? And if he's that stupid, how stupid am I for robbing a bank for him?"

"Ma'am, I can help you here!" The teller was a squeaky white girl with a scarf tied around her neck.

"Christ Jesus, the window's open, you gonna go or what?" a man behind her shouted.

She looked at the teller again, her perky nose and pursed lips. She couldn't let this snob think she couldn't spell. Plus, the two cameras up by the ceiling corners were gunning for her, zooming in on her fingerprints. "Go ahead," she said to the man, and backed away from the line, slowly and carefully, as if the bank's marble floors were crawling with snakes. When she stepped outside, all of New York surrounded her—the traffic, the radios, the pedestrians jamming the streets as the sun winked on their sunglasses and windshields and hot dog carts made of aluminum. Knowledge stood in the middle of it all and waited for the universe to confirm her decision. It only took a minute. A cabdriver screeched his brakes and cussed her out. She was dazed and crossing the street. "You coulda been killed!" the cigar-mouth said, and that was enough of a message. Yes, she could've been killed, and there was no way she was going to lose her life for some idiot who couldn't spell money. She had worked too hard to go down like that. She had standards.

After thanking the cabbie she treated herself to a slice of pepperoni and hopped onto a train that did not take her to the bathroom at Grand Central where her boyfriend was waiting.

Knowledge had standards.

She had principles. No one ever understood what they were exactly but at least she had them. It was her principles that ran after the thief to get the woman's wallet back. And it was her principles that had him trapped in the middle of the street, in the center of a small crowd, backing up the one-way traffic. By the time I caught up to them, Knowledge was circling the man like a boxer in a ring.

"Empty your pockets!" she ordered, and he did as told, pulling out the white tongues of his jean pockets to show he had nothing except lint and tobacco shreds.

"What's going on?" I asked, my breath short from the run.

"What the fuck you looking at!" she screamed at the man. "Take off your shirt!"

Her voice sounded different, lower than usual but also bright with adrenaline. The man dropped his white tee to the ground and someone in the crowd whistled.

"Turn around!" she yelled, and it dawned on me that she sounded like her father or stepfather or whatever he was, the one who'd caught us stealing his Christmas tree.

The man held his arms out and pinwheeled slowly, his sweaty chest covered in snails of black hair. He was maybe in his forties, with patches of gray along the sides of his bumpy Afro. He didn't look scared as much as exhausted from having run seven blocks with a morally strict girl chasing after him. I looked over at Knowledge. She wasn't even close to being out of breath.

"Maybe you're taking this a little too far?" I whispered.

"Too far?" She gripped her hips, looked at me straight, and then her stare slowly drifted to somewhere behind me. "I'm just getting started," she said, and as if my comment had sparked more authority in her, she commanded the guy to take off his pants.

"Uh-uh. No way," the man said, shaking his head.

Knowledge charged his face, and with the volume increasing with each and every word, she said, "Take— your fucking—pants off—now!"

Maybe the guy had thought she was an off-duty cop. Maybe Knowledge looked to him like an underaged narc. Or maybe he had grown up with a father who yelled just like her. Who knew why, with a crowd of twenty or so people watching him, he let a seventeen-year-old black girl from the Bronx convince him to unbutton his jeans, unzip his fly, and drop his pants so they bunched by his ankles, showing the corners of Twenty-second and Third his grim and sluggish underwear.

And nothing else.

"Where is it?" Knowledge demanded to know.

"You have to believe me. I have no idea what you're talking about." The man's voice rattled with frustration. "I was just walking and you came after me, with that look on your face and—"

"Oh shit," some kid said in the crowd, bordering on laughter. "She got the wrong guy."

Knowledge was crushed. The look on her face had morphed from righteousness to doubt to stunned disbelief. She turned to me, and I knew she was asking if I thought she had the wrong guy. He was definitely older than I'd thought he'd be, and kind of out of shape to be a mugger.

"It's by his foot! Under the jeans!" somebody shouted, and before Knowledge could investigate, the man hiked up his pants and broke through the crowd, leaving behind one fat wallet the size of a fist. Knowledge didn't run after him. She simply walked up to the wallet, picked it up, and looked at it. I was young then and hadn't yet discovered what it felt like to be proud of someone. The city was filled with cops and lawyers and officials who were supposed to help people in need, and there was Knowledge—a pusher, a transient, a wealth of misdemeanors—standing in the middle of the street as a crime fighter.

"So, what did we learn today," she asked me.

"Trust your instincts."

"Wrong. Stay in shape 'cause you never know when you have to kick some ass. Okay, what else."

"Help people when they're in need."

"Wrong again. Help *only* strangers. You can't go around helping all your friends 'cause they start depending on you and that gets you nowhere, okay?"

"Got it. Be good, but only to strangers."

Knowledge laughed and shook her head. "People think they're being good just 'cause they mow the lawn when their wives tell 'em," she said, loud enough for all to hear. "Or they give money to church when they got money in the bank. That's got nothing to do with good. Let's see how generous they are when their pockets are empty. You get what I'm saying?"

I nodded. The crowd loosened. They were fools. They weren't ready to hear the truth.

"That's when you see character," she said, just to me. "Don't be fooled by personality. Anyone can have a good personality. Shit, a dog can have a good personality. But God don't give a shit about that. He judges character. And he judges you during wartime, when you're in action, when you're down in the trenches. Not when you're sitting at home, drinking tea."

A cab pulled up at the corner and out came the woman from Union Square. I pointed this out to Knowledge. She was too busy staring at the wallet in her hand. "I'm gonna be saved," she said, and looked to me. "I'm gonna be saved."

The woman waddled up to us. "Oh, thank goodness. We've been driving up and down..."

Knowledge, with genuine pride, handed the wallet over. Somebody clapped. The crowd had dwindled down to maybe ten or so, diehards who wanted to see the ending.

"Here." The woman opened her wallet. "Let's give you something, a little reward."

Knowledge held up her hand. "We're all good. Thanks is thanks enough."

"But you have to take something. I insist," the woman said, fingering some cash.

"Really. I said your thanks is enough. So why don't you just say thank you, and we'll get moving."

"I don't know why you're taking that tone with me. I *am* trying to thank you."

Looking to the side, Knowledge cleaned her ear with an index finger.

"I see nothing wrong with giving people money, especially when they deserve it."

"I'll take your money," a construction worker said.

"Listen, lady." Knowledge braced the woman's arm. "You gonna say thank you or what?"

The woman snapped her arm back. "Who do you think you—"

Knowledge leaned in and whispered, "The next two words out of your mouth need to be: Thank. You."

"Like I said—"

Right away, Knowledge snatched the wallet from the woman's hands. "I warned you," she said, and walked off.

"She's got my wallet!" the woman screamed but nobody stopped Knowledge.

This image of her strutting down the block came back to me when our paths crossed in a Kentucky Fried Chicken, years after we'd lost each other. Knowledge worked in the back, her hands drowning and shaking a fryer basket of meat. The fade in her uniform told me she'd been working there awhile. The scabs on her face told me she was using now. I was, too, but I hadn't plunged as deep as she had. That's what I told myself anyway. I'd never seen her so thin. Her body seemed empty of flesh and fluids, and she was missing really important things, like her two front teeth. I was getting a bucket of wings for me and Benny, a guy I couldn't stop dating. I didn't call out to her. We hadn't seen each other for five hundred years. Too long to catch up properly with a counter between us. Plus, she wouldn't have wanted me to see her that way. So deflated, and so lost, shriveling inside that uniform of hers, the only thing holding her body together.

But on that sunny afternoon, Knowledge walked tall and proud down Third Avenue, her back as straight as a skyscraper.

"That was amazing," I said, catching up to her.

"I know," she said, sounding surprised herself. "I wanna see but I don't want to turn around. Is the crowd still there?"

I looked back. The street had returned to its normal pace—the sun and the cars and the people had erased the event. Even the woman was gone.

"They're all still there, watching you walk away."

"As they should be," she said, picking up her stride. "As they should be."

At some point we stopped at a trash can. Before Knowledge tossed the wallet, she pulled the cash, gave me a twenty, and shoved the rest in her pocket. "Sometimes you gotta do wrong to do right, know what I'm saying?"

"Now I do."

"That's my girl," she said, and the smile on her face lasted for two blocks.

On the Bus

One time I rode a bus that ran a red light and crashed into a family wagon, killing the baby in the backseat.

But before that, I sat with my face out the window, letting the sun zap the ants crawling behind my eyes. Two days of speeding, bagging, drinking crème de menthe, and snorting procaine, and now it was daylight, and the worms were already digging into my skin. The guy sitting next to me bit into a soggy taco. The smell of wet beef made me want to vomit.

And then I saw him. Two seats down, with his back to the window. An old black man with sky-bright eyes who smiled at everyone as though he'd seen all of them as children once. He looked familiar. Bald head, white beard, skin darker than grapes. His uniform overalls had a stitched name tag that had no name, and the mop next to him was new, its head still wrapped in plastic. He could've been a janitor, but I'd never seen one ride around with a mop, or look so happy doing it. He nodded and beamed at everyone. Until he turned to me. With his hands on his lap, he stared into me as if to light me on fire.

That's when we slammed head-on into the station wagon.

Someone screamed, Oh God! just before the crash, which sounded like a thousand knives being sharpened all at once. People lunged forward and then back, landing on their ribs, their cheeks. Apples, celery, and canned beans rolled on the floor, and an old lady's walker slammed into the fare machine. On his knees, a man in a suit gathered the papers that had spilled from his briefcase, not hearing the girl next to him crying for her doll. It felt good to hear the bus come to life. It calmed me to see them acting out what I felt inside. Some tried to push open the doors, others hugged, and others cried into their hands, their fingers wiping their eyes. But the black man—he hadn't budged. He was still facing me. Even his mop hadn't moved. That's when I knew he was God. He'd come for me but the baby had gotten in the way.

Behind the driver's seat, a Puerto Rican woman

cried and rubbed her round stomach, and sitting on the floor in the aisle, an old man screamed of a broken arm but nobody but me understood because he was crying in Korean. With all this going on, the black man finally stood up and held out his hand. "Come with me," he said, still without a smile, and I knew exactly what he meant. He had long, dark hands with pinkish knuckles. I'd never been so scared. My heart tightened. "Come on," he said, but I shook my head and told him I wasn't ready to go with him. He left through the rear door.

A little while later, I realized everybody had evacuated the bus.

Outside I stumbled past the ambulance, the fire trucks, the emergency people hovering around the mother who was busy wiping down her child. The asphalt was a lace of sparkling diamonds—a beautiful, jagged doily for the crushed picnic basket, the soggy bib, the map stuck to the pavement with sticky blood. I searched for the janitor. I wanted to see where he would go. I even looked for him up in the sky, blinding myself until everything vanished

I used to think my father was God.

That was before I'd found him passed out drunk at

the Derby Motel. His Lincoln was parked in front of his room, and the manager peeked through the window blinds before unlocking the door for me.

"He has the stomach flu," I said, walking in.

The manager stayed outside. "I understand," he said, and closed the door.

The air smelled acidic. Something about that smell and the heat made me think he might be dead. He wasn't. A blanket sat crumpled in the middle of the bed in a large hill, and my father lay on top of it with his back arched, his nose hissing, a newspaper tenting his chest. The TV was on. Moldy cartons of Chinese food pegged the sheets, and on the nightstand paper-bagged bottles, four of them, towered behind an ashtray jammed with cigarette butts. The smell of the room hurt my head, but at least I had found him. It was my job to get him back. Sometimes he made it easy by leaving behind clues. A ticket stub from the dry cleaners where he had a mistress. Sticks of coffee-flavored gum from a Korean restaurant, where he had another. This time, it was the Yellow Pages opened to a listing of motels, and I picked the one closest to our house.

I climbed onto the bed and rattled his arm. "Appa, wake up."

He had on a white undershirt, Bermuda shorts—the ones I'd given him for Father's Day—and black dress shoes with the laces undone. The shoes confused me; I didn't understand why he had them on. They were his show-off shoes, the ones he'd worn to church or to the bank for a loan. He'd put on that exact pair to take his citizenship test at the immigration office some months back, and while we waited out in the hallway for his name to be called, he spit shined the shoes with newspaper. I was coaching him on U.S. history and asked who our first president was. He said George Washington Bridge, and then laughed at his mistake. I'd loved him more than anything in the world right then.

Some time after the bus ride, I got into a fight with Knowledge. We were standing on our corner—Derek pushing his gold watches (wrapped six on each arm and two on each skinny ankle), Grunt dumpster-diving in the alley behind Donut King, and Reverend LeRoy standing on top of his fake alligator skin briefcase, hugging his Bible and forgiving our sins. "It is a beautiful, sunny day," he said, "a glorious day that sheds light on your unsavory lives for God to see and judge. You are afflicted, my children, with a poverty and abandonment Jesus suffered all his life." The reverend also mentioned that he'd been a junkie before he found God. But considering that he had OD'd once and almost died, my guess was that God had found him first. *You go too far and the Lord will come looking for you*, my mother said once. Wink was there, too, working across the street, sticking his head into cars and his ass up in the air, holding up traffic while trying to pick up johns. All kinds of men pulled over for him—a few grizzlies with lumberjack shirts, a few elbow patches, some neckties, and a lot of geezers with skin like pork rinds. Wink hated every one of them but he could always count on them showing up. He told me they were the only things he could count on.

It was my fifteenth birthday and Knowledge wouldn't treat me to a nickel bag. Her buyers came up left and right, sliding money into her hands, but she wouldn't let go of one lousy bag, not even to me. She told me she'd seen me hooking and I said, "So," and she said she didn't *associate* with no hos. That was a lie. She was jealous because I had a boyfriend. "You're pissed because I never let you eat me," I yelled at her, maybe for the first time. That got everyone's attention. Derek stopped selling watches to cheer me on, "Aww shit, girl, you tell that bitch!"

Knowledge told him to shut the fuck up, and then faced me, saying how I had changed. "You're getting strung out on the shit," she said, calling me a slut this and slut that.

"Skanky ass cheap dyke," I called back. As soon as I said it, I felt I had been poisoned and it was the poison saying these words to my only true friend, in the middle of the street no less.

She didn't get mad, which frightened me. She just shook her head and waved me over. "Look." She leaned in and clutched the back of my neck. "I'm giving you one bag, but that's it. You're so fucked on this shit," she said, looking far down the street. "You ain't turned out like I taught you."

I nodded, I apologized. "You're right," I told her. "You're the only one who knows me."

"You can't forget that," she said, and I said I wouldn't.

After making sure there weren't any cops, she said we should hit the alley. I was glad that she was giving in, but even happier that she wanted to get high with me, something she rarely did. In the alley, we knelt behind the dumpster where I usually smoked. From inside her panties, she pulled out a baggie and dangled it in front of me. It felt good to see it so close. "You want this?" she asked, and punched me in the mouth. My head banged metal. I was about to look up when she grabbed me in a headlock. With the crook of her arm, she wrenched my neck and kept shouting, "Go ahead, say again what you called me. C'mon, say it."

"It's my birthday!" I reminded her.

She finally let go and flexed her arm. I rubbed my throat.

"Well, happy fucking birthday then," she said, and kicked my thigh before leaving.

A part of me was glad to see her go, but then I was alone. Resting my head against the wall, I watched something crawl up and into the dumpster. I had bitten my tongue. My mouth tasted like spoons. On birthdays you were supposed to get gifts and cake and people were supposed to be nice to you. We used to be good friends, Knowledge and me. I wondered what had happened.

Later on I found out that Knowledge was jealous of Philly, my first boyfriend. Philly was an artist and I fell in love with him because he had brown eyes that always looked wet. He worked part-time as a rink guard at Skate World, and I only saw him during his shifts because he said we couldn't hang out at his loft. He was forty-two. "I don't want my neighbors talking. You'd be fine, but I could get into a shitload of trouble," he'd said, smiling, his hand smoothing my back.

When we first met, I'd been afraid to tell him my age, thinking he would turn me in to the police, but he assured me that he didn't mind me being fourteen, that he would love me no matter what. Tuesdays and Thursdays were usually our nights at the rink, and he always bought me hot chocolate and a cookie if I wanted. And when no one was looking, I would sneak into one of the ballet rooms, still with my skates on, where professional skaters like Tai Babilonia and Randy Gardner practiced their moves on the ground. At least, that was what Philly had told me. He would come in a little while after, and we would lie in the dark under the ballet bar with the mirror behind us, his red satin Skate World jacket pillowing our heads. We'd kiss softly and fuck and the hard floor didn't hurt because being there was better than being in some car with a date. I couldn't even compare Philly to a date, and I didn't care about his age, his gray hair, or the potbelly.

"Do you love me?" I asked him once.

"Sure I do."

"Why?"

"What do you mean why."

"Don't you have a reason?"

"Sure. I got a reason," he said, rolling over to light a cigarette. "Because you're a rose in a field of dirty old tires, that's why."

He always talked like that, as if he would've died if I hadn't come to rescue him. After sex we'd smoke a line to pick us up, and for the rest of the night I'd skate circles around him, bending over to show him my panty under my skirt, knowing he'd fantasize about that for a week.

After my fight with Knowledge, I went to see him. We celebrated my birthday by snorting a ton of meth and drinking bourbon from his flask. I was glad he didn't ask about the bruise on my lips, even though I knew he'd noticed. He hadn't gotten me a present but I told myself that that was okay because we fucked and held each other long and he got me higher than I'd ever been. Gifts seemed silly compared to that kind of exchange. When we finished he put on his jacket, the satin still glossy even in the dark, and left the room. After waiting a few minutes—about twenty bottles of beer on the wall—I went back out onto the rink. The shock of white light surrounded me whole and I couldn't feel anything but loved. I floated above the ice and my eyes softened, eased into reality, into colors, then shapes, then outlines, and gradually focused on smiling lips, pom-pom gloves, and finally on Philly, skating at the far end of the rink, with another girl.

She was wearing his jacket. Her arms were touching the insides of his sleeves, sucking up all of his leftover warmth. And under his jacket—she had on a white turtleneck and a white miniskirt that made her look like a slut cheerleader. She was older than me, maybe eighteen or nineteen, which meant he could take her to his loft without getting in trouble. He held her hands and skated backwards with too much tenderness, and she clung to him, pretending she might fall any second. She was a liar and a trashy whore. She just wanted him to hold her.

Before I could think about it, I was skating hockey-style toward them. I cut across traffic and the center coned section, and slammed into them. They hadn't seen me coming and we all fell—Philly on his butt, the girl on her face. I jumped her back and punched her in the head and the spine of her neck, forgetting everything Knowledge had taught me and just letting my arms swing as if they'd been wound up to do exactly that. I thought I could fight mountains and whales, until the beauty of crystal meth wavered for a second, just long enough for Philly and another rink guard to pull me off. They dragged me to a bench and told me to stay put. I didn't know what had come over me but was glad it had passed. "Who the fuck is she?" I asked Philly, but he left me to see about the girl. People crowded around her. I could only see her pink legs spread out on the ice.

Then it was my turn, I guess. Two or three guys came out of nowhere, pushed me to the ground, and started punching. I didn't close my eyes, though. I looked up at each and every one of them as their fists zoomed in and hit my nose, my cheeks, my brows. When one was done, another got on so they could all take a shot. This time the rink guards weren't so quick to the rescue. I'd been beaten up before, so it wasn't a big deal. Sometimes, if you were down long enough, some wire in your brain got snipped and all the noise just vanished. And when the sound left, the pain left, too, leaving you flat on the floor, watching a peaceful movie of yourself taking every hit and feeling absolutely nothing. During those times, I was a superhero.

When the sound came back on, the guys were walking away, turning only to throw their soda cans and half-eaten candy bars at my head. I spat in their direction, even reached for a can and threw it back at them except I knew my anger meant nothing to them. Philly was nowhere. I guess that hurt the most. It killed me to think that he was with that girl—that she would get to be in his home. All the kids stared at me, wanting to know some secret about me. I thought about running into the bathroom and cutting my wrists with the jagged toe-stops on my skates. Then I thought about just standing up.

Later on, a rink guard told me that the girl was Philly's niece and that he had taken her to the hospital. She was visiting from West Virginia and had come to the rink with some boys from her cheerleading squad.

Same time of day, same stop. I got on the bus again, having told no one about having seen God. If the news had gotten out, undeserving people would crowd the bus and I'd never see him again. This time, I was ready to go with. I had nothing left to give, and nothing anyone would want to take. My seat at the back corner of the bus was empty, so I sat there, hoping he would come, especially since I'd made sure not to be too high but just high enough to where I could stay still and not have my skin moving. I looked around in case he was there but had on a different disguise, but the only black person was an old blind woman up at the front.

God didn't show that day, but one of his angels did.

She was maybe five years old with lemony hair, and she sat alone, three seats to my right. That was how I knew she was special. Five-year-olds in Sunday dresses didn't sit in the back of the bus by themselves. That, and she held in her hands an egg timer, the kind that looked like a mini sundial. It was white, like her dress and stockings and shoes. She pretended to ignore me and I kept silent, not wanting to seem too desperate. The sunlight around her looked crisp and icy. I slid over a seat to feel its temperature.

"Do you want more time?" she asked, sighing as if she had asked this an hour ago and I had failed to answer. I looked down the bus to see if anyone else had heard her. Nobody had. The bus gurgled and made a sharp turn.

"No." I bent toward her. "I mean, no thank you. I don't want any more time here, I want to go with you." I said this quietly and slowly, convinced we were being recorded somehow.

She rolled her eyes and drooped her shoulders. Winding up the timer, she said, "Well, I'm going to give you more time anyway. See?" She held it out in front of me. Twenty. Nineteen. Eighteen. The ticking reminded me of rats climbing into dumpsters, their claws clacking metal. I couldn't hear myself think, so I snatched the timer from her.

"I told you already, I don't want any more time here," I said, as nicely as I could, while trying to turn the damn thing off. But then she screamed. How such a tiny pink mouth could be so loud! Like she was screaming from an old memory, buried in my head. She screeched and cried, her pale face melting like plastic in a trash fire, and I said sorry, over and over again, and tried to give back the timer but she wouldn't take it. So I pulled her wrist, unfisted her hand, and placed the timer in her palm, which made her shriek even louder. She flung it onto the floor. Everyone turned to us, even the blind woman, but I couldn't care about them. I just wanted her to shut up. I put my fingers over her mouth, just to shush her, but then a woman came and snatched her away. I didn't see where she'd come from. Her enormous head shouted things at me, things I couldn't hear because all I heard was the angel screaming. Then the bus stopped and they both got off. Nobody asked me to come along.

How much longer did I have to wait for Him? To get his attention?

My father was so drunk I couldn't wake him. His shorts were soiled and the flies in the room flew crooked into walls, quiet attempts at suicide. They had nothing on us. They didn't know how much pain we could withstand. I tried to clean up the room a little. Floating in the tub were several cigarette butts and one chopstick. His wallet was in the sink, his belt over the towel rack, and his car keys were under the toilet, next to a wet pile he'd thrown up. After I finished in the bathroom I took a dollar from his wallet and got a root beer from the motel soda machine. The can cooled my palms, so I pressed it against my ear and rolled it across my forehead and neck. When I came back, I turned off the TV, popped open the soda, hopped onto the bed, and tried to wake him again. The flies buzzed over the garbage can, over the tall bottles of vodka. Seeing my father on the bed like that made me realize how he was both weak and strong—weak enough to drink so much yet strong enough to still be alive.

I held the soda over his head and let a few beads of condensation drip onto his eyelids until he eventually opened them. He saw me and told me to go back home. I told him I couldn't do that. He'd been gone a week this time and Mom's sleepwalking had gotten worse. It had become tiring, guarding her door every night and following her into the kitchen to make sure she didn't cut herself chopping scallions for an hour. I tried rolling my father over but couldn't, so I placed my cold palm on his forehead and told him that he had to come home, that he couldn't leave me alone with her. "She's sick," I said, "and she's not interested in me." My father snatched the root beer and flung it behind me, the can smacking into the wall and spewing a froth of browns. Then he lay back down, saying he wasn't interested in anybody.

It was a perfect night. I knew it was cold by the way the other girls were dressed in jackets and gloves, but my skin felt as warm as pancakes. I straightened my tube top, hiked up my miniskirt, and pinched up my fishnets.

"Hi." I ran up to the car window before anyone else could take him. "Welcome to McDonald's." I smiled. "You wanna date?" The man seemed nice, almost cute, with a mustache like my sixth-grade homeroom teacher.

"Get in."

I opened the door and waved bye to the girls. The sluts gave me the finger. I couldn't blame them. I was on their block, taking tricks without paying Shades. *Pretty soon, he's gonna come for your ass*, they all said, but fuck Shades. I didn't care about him or the girls or what Knowledge or Philly thought of me, because right at that

moment, I was in a car that smelled like watermelon
Bubble Yum, sitting on sheepskin seats and feeling love
from a blasting heater. My date slapped in an eight-track.
The theme song from *Fame* came on.

"You see this movie?" He took off his wedding ring,
dropped it into his shirt pocket, where he pulled out a
Binaca.

"Yeah," I told him. "I snuck into it and saw it five
times. It was great."

He spritzed the Binaca twice. Just like him, the car
was too clean. Nothing on the dash, nothing in the back
except two bags of groceries. I told him his car was boring. He didn't laugh or anything, just said, "Oh yeah?"
and kept driving. Even his plaid shirt and his pants looked
like they'd just been ironed. Through the speakers, Irene
Cara sang, *I'm gonna live forever. I'm gonna learn how to
fly.* I turned up the volume and noticed dangling on the
tuner knob a small cross with a pretty silver Jesus.

"How old are you anyway?" he asked, fixing the rear-
view mirror.

I plucked the cross, looked at it, felt the tiny bump of a
nail in his feet. "I don't know, how old you want me to be?"

He took the cross from my hands and dropped it in
his shirt pocket.

"You look like you could be my daughter's age."

The car made a turn. I could see the motel sign halfway down the block. "Is that who you want me to be?" I said and leaned in, my chin on his shoulder, my hand on his leg.

"Sure," he said, looking at the road. "You can be my kid."

With a Boy

I lived on the sixth floor of an abandoned building with a boy who worked, like me. Blue Fly, with his sunny hair and pool-blue eyes, sold himself mostly. He stayed away for days, one time a whole week, and he almost always came back with money and a boil somewhere on his body. When he wasn't hooking or shooting heroin, he snuck clothes out of Laundromats and sold them on sidewalks miles away with a cardboard poster that said: GARAGE SALE, MOVING TO ALASKA. He stole everything, all the time, and the closer we got, the more he stole from me. He had a thing for keys, and my money. But being with him was easy, and once in a while we loved each other as if God himself had taught us how.

But then the accident happened. He was on the floor,

cooking his spoon over the Sterno can, and I was mad because he'd said there was only enough for him—that half would do neither of us any good. He tapped his favorite vein, the one he called the Great Wall of China, and I kicked the Sterno out from under him. He should've moved, most people would've, but he was so focused on his arm, so stubborn about rolling his eyes backwards and falling into the rush, he didn't care about the small fire clinging to his leg. His back sloped against the wall. His eyes turned to worms. I stood there watching him nodding and half-swatting his calf before realizing that maybe I should help.

At the hospital, under the white lights and in front of a pretty nurse with tired eyes, Blue Fly spit in my face. His leg was wet-bandaged and slung up by the ankle, and the nurse was touching his knee in a way I didn't much like. Then Blue called me a useless stupid cunt. I was relieved that he was finally talking to me, but instead of saying that, I punched him in the stomach and called him a faggot junkie. "You sell your asshole," I screamed, which made the nurse hold her hands up at me. "That's it, visiting hour's over," she said, pushing me out the door. I told her she should hold on to her keys.

In the hallway I walked past a line of beds lumped with sick people, their gowns too thin to hide their fears. I wasn't bothered by the honesty of it all. My mom worked as a midnight nurse at a very busy hospital. Once when I was young, I asked her what she did for a living. She told me she saved people she didn't care about.

That night, I slept on the train until a cop poked me with his stick. I got up, said sorry to his baton, and switched trains, then switched again, until it finally turned morning. At rush hour, I started work as usual.

Me, I didn't sell myself anymore—I sold newspapers. Not like a paper route where you hopped on your bike at six in the morning, but like fishing out pages from the trash can and selling them on the trains when metro cops weren't looking. The key was to screen the pages good, make sure there weren't any coffee blots or footprints. It was a job. I didn't beg. Panhandling was for losers.

On good days, I'd make eight or ten bucks and sometimes people handed money over without even taking a page, maybe thinking their donation would keep their kids from turning out like me.

With a Boy

After picking through a few bins I stepped into a packed car. The morning was hot and gluey, and people on the train looked to be heading to a funeral, their heads too heavy for their shoulders. Even the air felt thicker, harder to swallow. I held up a page and squeezed between sweating bodies, my elbow rubbing against the backs of business suits, selling news about Mark David Chapman's sentencing. "Gets twenty-years-to-life," I yelled, over the train noise. No one looked up. "Reads *Catcher in the Rye* in court," I said, tapping the page, but still nobody heard me. A chill spread up my neck and behind my ears, making me salivate. My stomach cramped. I hadn't had a hit in two days—if you don't count shooting up water—and my body felt invaded by electric eels. Looking for more space, I moved to the back. "Love pulled the trigger," I said, under my breath, suddenly wanting to give up everything I'd ever known for an empty seat, or to see Blue. In my head I spelled out his name, over and over, but then wasn't sure if I'd been talking out loud. The car smelled of cooked cheese. The weight of others kept me standing as I closed my eyes and imagined giant hands wringing my body clean. It had been a while since I'd taken a day off. I thought about playing hooky, maybe taking a trip out to the ocean. I could take the train there and ride like a regular passenger, like everybody else, except I'd smile at people and pretend I was their summer sun.

I threw up in the station bathroom. It splattered every-where, some of it hitting the toilet water and splashing back onto my face. I rinsed off in one of those sinks that had a single faucet you pushed to get water, making it impossible to wash your face using both hands. With my shirtsleeve I wiped off a mirror tagged with so much graffiti I couldn't see any of me.

Later that day, while working near the token booth, I saw them. The nurse from the hospital, with Blue Fly. They passed me and didn't even notice. She had her arm around him, and even though they were a few people ahead of me, I could tell he wasn't limping anymore. The bitch nurse had healed his leg already. I couldn't stand the thought of Blue going to this woman's home. All this time I'd thought he only did men, old ugly men with warts on their fingers, but now I saw he'd been cheat-ing on me all along. From her he'd get money, food, new clothes, and who knew what else, maybe even a car. She probably had a pool. Under the exit sign, she stopped to run her fingers through his hair, just above the back of his neck. That's when I decided to follow them.

Outside, the sun was so bright you couldn't even see it, and the heat dried the blood in my veins, making me want to dig them out with my fingernails. But I was freezing, too. I hugged myself and sweated and followed them anyway, down a busy street dotted with garbage bags, a quieter street bouncing with a game of stickball, a block of skinny houses, a row of hedges, then into a short driveway lined with potted plants. And it wasn't until I found a safe spot behind a tree in her backyard that I realized that the boy wasn't Blue. He was actually someone I'd never seen in my life. His hair wasn't even blond. Through the sliding glass doors, I watched the nurse talking to this boy, who I now guessed was her son, although she looked too young to be his mother. They talked for a while as she opened and closed the refrigerator door, setting food on the counter. I imagined their conversation to be very boring.

Then for no good reason the boy came outside. I ducked down behind the tree.

"Hello?" His voice came closer. "Who's there?"

Closing my eyes seemed like the thing to do.

"Hello?" he said again, and I made myself smaller, squeezing my eyes tighter. "I'm standing right in front of you, you know."

A tall skinny boy who wasn't more than twelve stood in front of me, all right, holding a Rubik's Cube. I couldn't believe I'd thought he was Blue.

"Mom! There's an Oriental girl in our yard! Mom!"

I thought about telling him that I was at the wrong house but decided to just head for the gate. It was too late, though. The nurse came out, dish towel over one shoulder. Tilting her head, she tried to remember me, tried to place me between good and evil.

"I think she's a street person, Mom."

"Alex, please."

"Well, she could be. Maybe she doesn't speak English," he said, and shouted, "Are—you—home—less?"

In a strange way, I liked the way he was talking to me. He was so interested, like I was a science project I truly believed in. I didn't say a word, though, afraid I might break the spell.

"Maybe we should bring her in," he said.

. . .

In the shower, I uncapped all the different shampoos the nurse owned and sniffed each and every one of them. One was called Monterey Mist. Another, Australian Kiwi. The smells made me hungry. I was getting ready to lather up the washcloth when a hand poked through the curtains.

"Here," she said, handing me a kitchen sponge. "You can use this."

I took it, held it flat in my hand, wondered if it was new or little used or if any of that mattered. The sponge made me think of something that had happened on a train a while back. A woman had sat staring up at me in a way I was sure was rude. She had dry hair and small bird eyes and was wearing a T-shirt that said *#1 Nana* in glitter paint. I'd decided she was an unhappy person. But not knowing what to make of her really, I asked if she wanted a page.

She said nothing and kept staring.

"They're today's pages," I told her, and showed her one, but her eyes wouldn't blink. I wanted to snap her head off.

"You can't die from talking to me," I whispered to her, and as if someone had put coins into her slot, her face cringed. I was winning. She was going to speak, her lips were going to move and she was going to talk to me as if I were a real person, and I was ready to prove to her that she wasn't better, just better off.

"You smell," she said.

The nurse had put out a shirt, hospital pants, and mismatched socks on top of the toilet seat. Without drying off I jumped into the clothes and wiped the steam off the mirror so I could see the new me. The hair was tangled and everything fit a little loose, but I wished Blue was there.

In the kitchen she stood over the stove, stirring ketchup into a pan of meat.

"Hi," I said, from the other side of the counter.

"Christ, you scared me."

I apologized.

The light above her drew tired shadows on her face. I wanted to thank her right then, to tell her that no stranger had ever been this good to me, but then we both sort of looked away and the moment turned old. She pulled out a bottle from the freezer and made herself a drink.

"Where's your kid?" I asked.

"He's at the neighbor's."

"Oh."

She took a sip and folded her arms. "How was the shower?"

"Good."

"That's good," she said.

"The shampoos were real nice."

She rearranged a magnet on the fridge. "Oh, you used those? Good. I'm glad."

"How's Blue Fly?" I asked.

"Who?"

"My boyfriend. At the hospital."

"Oh. That's where I know you from. You're ... what's his face ... Walter's friend."

I didn't think she deserved to know his real name.

"He's good," she said. "At least when I left him he was."

On the side of the fridge hung a calendar of famous nurses. That month was Miss Dorothea Dix, a Civil War nurse. "You know my mom's a—"

I stopped talking because the woman dumped her

drink into a blender and pushed a button, and then another.

"Look, I'd ask you to stay for dinner but...I'm sorry, did you say something?"

"That's okay. I'm actually not that hungry. I should get going," I said, opening the sliding glass door.

"Hey, how about some money?" She looked around the kitchen. "Do you want some money?" From under the counter she pulled out a Yellow Pages and opened it to a section stuffed with bills. "Shit. I only have six dollars."

I told her it was okay, that I didn't want any.

"What're you talking about?" She put the six bucks on the counter between us, and I noticed that her hand was shaking. "I'd give you more, but who the hell knows where my purse is," she said, her hand clutching a clump of her bangs. "My whole life was in there."

After I left the woman's house, I went to the hospital where my mother worked. From behind a bush I watched cars pull up the circular driveway and carry the sick home. The cherry light on top of an ambulance spun in the dark and the hospital windows turned black, one by one, as I waited for almost an hour. It was close to midnight when my mom finally came. I only saw her a few seconds—killing the cigarette on the sidewalk, brushing something off her uniform before walking through the automatic doors and then down a green striped hallway. She hadn't changed much since I had left her almost three years ago—her hair was still short, still blunt, still black. But maybe it was somebody else. It could've been. I don't know.

Blue was asleep when I got home that night. I reached up and turned on the flashlight he'd rigged so it hung from the ceiling. The floor turned into a pale yellow egg, and the light made pretty everything it touched—an open can of ravioli, the bandage just below his knee, a green leather purse. He'd fallen asleep in his underwear, the gear still in his arm. I knelt down and pulled it out as slowly as I could, but it wasn't easy—his skin and pus had dried around the needle. "I knew you'd come back," he said with a sleepy smile. I loved him so much then. "Anything left for me?" I asked. He pushed himself up slowly and kissed me on the lips. "Yeah," he said, and I leaned back against the wall, feeling my new clean body sink through the plaster as he rolled up my sleeve and placed his arm under mine. "That all right?" he asked, tightening the belt, finding the right notch, flicking the needle, then smoothing the skin on my arm, up and down—always so good at tracing my wire, always so good at taking me home. I closed my eyes and thought about the mother and the son and the tree and the train, and how one day could expand into a lifetime, then shrink again into one single moment.

"Ready?" Blue asked, and pushed before I could answer.

Avon

At night I used to ride the ferry back and forth, from the city to Staten Island. I'd watch the diamond lights smearing the wet window glass or stand out on the windy deck as the regulars sat crooked, drinking their pints and shouting about different kinds of loss. The engine shook my legs. The water pricked my skin. I stood on the railing and let the wind sting my eyes and tickle my veins where a warm drug bubbled through, heating up like the wires of an electric blanket. I was sixteen and pregnant then, thinking that the ups and downs of the East River would kill it somehow.

But that was at night.

During the day, I was an Avon Lady. I washed up, combed out the knots in my hair, put on the blouse and skirt I'd stolen from a Laundromat, and knocked on every apartment door I could find. I got the job by answering a newspaper ad that asked only for my money, and in return I received a brochure, two order books, and a pink sample case that carried all things pretty. Just looking at the samples made me want to wash my hands. Eye shadows came in tiny disks, looking like sour candies, lipsticks grew from towers of gold, and mini bottles of foundation stood perfectly straight and guarded the six shades of blush that lived in large metal squares. All the pieces fit so perfectly in their slots, as if they belonged there and nowhere else.

Avon was supposed to be my ticket out. I wanted to get straight. Save up money and get a place. I wasn't the best salesgirl but I liked the job—I liked being inside people's homes because there I wasn't pregnant, I wasn't a runaway, I wasn't using. With the makeup on I became a new version of me—a well-mannered Korean girl, who sat with her legs crossed in living rooms decorated with plastic-covered couches and plastic-covered lampshades. I smiled often. I spoke softly. I sold to housewives.

At first they'd act as if their schedules couldn't possibly include me, but within minutes they were showing me their wedding photos, the warts on their toes, the strands of foreign hair they'd found on their husbands' sweaters. They whined about rainy vacations or their selfish in-laws or how the pearls they'd gotten for Christmas didn't match the ones from Mother's Day. They pulled out dresses they'd bought and tried them on, and I said nothing about their asses looking like old pillows. I presented the benefits of hypoallergenics and how Bahamas Berry Blush could turn back their clocks. They recited the plotlines of *All My Children* and asked if I thought their no-good husbands were cheating on them. I said no because that was what they wanted to hear. And I said yes because that was what they wanted to hear.

Some purchased out of guilt. Some wasted my time. They'd talk to me as if I were their best friend, but when it came time to open their wallets, they dug their fingers in the samples, chewed on my pen, spilled coffee on my case, and used my order forms to jot down telephone messages, only to tell me at the very end that what they really needed was to go on a diet instead of buying cosmetics. Then go on a fucking diet, I'd think and take something of theirs before I left—a music box, a photo, a wedding ring stuck in a soap dish.

. . .

This was my last building for the night. I knocked on a door even though dinnertime had long passed.

"Who is it?" a boy asked. He sounded ten or eleven.

"It's the Avon Lady."

"What?"

"The Avon Lady," I shouted into the crack of the door, probably loud enough for the whole building to hear.

"You're kidding. Hey, Ma! Guess what! It's the Avon Lady, like the commercials!" The boy laughed at his joke.

Waiting for the mother to open up, I glanced down at my pink case and realized that Avon spelled backwards was Nova. Reading upside down made me queasy. They shouldn't call it morning sickness if it happens all day. A few minutes went by. Nobody came to the door. I knocked on the next apartment.

"Nobody home!" a woman shouted.

"Okay, but you can't say that because I can hear you."

"Sorry. Nobody home!" she said again.

On my notepad I scribbled the last two apartment numbers so I knew to bug them again tomorrow. A woman came up the stairs then, passed me in the hallway, and stopped two units down. She knocked, and after a little while she began whispering into the door. I worried she was also selling. She was blond and dressed in matching lavender. I couldn't compete with lavender. My skirt, the color of sidewalk, hung loose around my waist, enough to be spun around, and my knee-highs crept down my calves with my every step. Everything on the lavender woman was fitted, and everything matched. She wasn't carrying anything except a hat and an umbrella, though. No merchandise meant she couldn't be in sales, so I eased up and moved on to the next apartment.

"Get away from the door!" a man shouted between coughing fits.

"I have Wild Country aftershave if you'd like to—"

"You don't leave, I'm calling the fucking cops!"

I took out my notepad: *Apt. 3C = man, mean, cops.* I took a deep breath and reminded myself of the Avon sales motto: *The more NOs you get, the better the odds of the next one being a YES.* The slogan made no sense but I couldn't help but believe it. As I was putting my notepad away, I caught the lavender woman staring at me. She had seen me getting yelled at, getting rejected, so I looked to her, to tell her that it wasn't a big deal and that this sort of stuff came with the territory. What I didn't expect was for her to come toward me.

"I'm done," she said.

By the time I thought to ask her what she meant, she was already on the first-floor landing, pulling her hat down tight and readying her umbrella for the weather outside.

I stared at the doorway where she'd stood. The apartment numbers were long gone but the paint still held the shadow of 3D. I walked up to the door, looked around, and listened to what sounded like choir music, a high wispy note ghosting through the walls. I raised my hand to give a knock until the rosary caught my eye. Wooden beads, faded and cracked, wrapped twice around the doorknob. It didn't belong there. Neither did the birdhouse nailed above the peephole. Or maybe it was a cuckoo clock. Whatever it was, green painted-on vines swarmed the wooden walls, the tin roof, and the tiny door, which was dotted by a doorknob the size of a grape seed. I touched the knob, feeling like a doll too big for her dollhouse.

"Who is it?"

I snapped my hand back. It was a woman's voice. "Hi, I'm the Avon Lady," I said, into the peephole.

"Oh, that's lovely." Her voice was high and breathy. I pictured an old twig of a grandmother on the other side. "I'm Sister Janine."

"Okay," I said, noticing the rosary again, the gaps between the beads. "Listen, maybe I should come back tomorrow? It's getting late and I'm sure you—"

"It's only eight-thirty. We have time before *Hart to Hart* comes on."

"If you say so." I pulled up my knee-highs, gripped the handle of my case with both hands, straightened my posture, and waited for her to open up. Somebody in the building was making popcorn. And somebody started playing scales on the piano.

"Whenever you're ready, I'm at your service," she said, but the door didn't budge.

I didn't understand. "I'm sorry...I usually show my samples, in person, you know, *inside* the apartments." When I said this, she giggled.

"Did I say something funny?"

"Oh, you mustn't think I'm ridiculing you."

Until she said this, I didn't think she was.

"This is your first time, isn't it?" she asked.

"Actually, I've been doing this for about a—"

"Best to just think of me as a telephone operator," she went on. "You never see the operator, right?"

I put my samples down. Getting her to open up was going to take some work.

"And that means I am not a body. I am a voice that connects you to God and nothing more. How long ago was your last confession?"

I stepped back. I checked behind me to see if someone was playing a trick. There was only a garbage chute and, below that, a broken turntable.

"Are you still there?" she asked.

"I think so."

I stared at the rosary and remembered the woman in lavender. *I'm done*, she'd said, as though I'd been waiting in line behind her.

"Are you Catholic?"

I thought about my parents' church. "No. Just a Presbyterian."

The eye of the peephole seemed to darken right then. "That's all right," she said. "I take all kinds."

I dropped to the ground and peered through a gap, about an inch thick, between the door and carpet. Pink fuzzy slippers paced back and forth. "I'm having a two-for-one sale on mascara right now, are you interested?" I got up and peeked into the peephole.

"...I'm your mother, your best friend, your lover, your therapist. I am whatever you need in order to open up to God. And it sounds like you really need to open up."

"I'm sorry?"

"I said, it sounds like you need to show your true self to God."

"You don't even know me." She was starting to piss me off.

"Don't be so sure."

"Well, then you should know that I'm fine," I said, as politely as possible.

"Of course you're fine, we're all fine. How about you, Mr. Coffee Table? Are you fine? I'm fine. And you, Miss Martini, you hanging in there? Because if you're fine, then I'm fine. We're all *fine*. But couldn't we be finer?"

She was taking my lines. That was what I told my customers when they tried to back out of a sale. They'd say, *I'm happy with my look,* and I'd say, *But don't you want to be happier?*

"I don't know what to tell you, but if you're not gonna buy something—"

"Here, a little handout for you," she said, and a pink flyer slid through the gap. It was titled "How to Confess," followed by step-by-step instructions. Step one read: *Forgive me, Sister, for I have sinned, it's been (insert length of time) since my last confession.* Step three said: *Whether your sins are mortal, venial, or slight imperfections, simply tell God all your troubles and you will be forgiven, guaranteed!*

"Are the instructions clear?"

"Absolutely," I said, backing away. "I'll be sure to come by tomorrow." I took out my notepad and wrote: *3D, crazy nun lady.*

"Well, we can start now if you'd like."

"I'll just take this home with me, to study it. Okay?"

She didn't answer.

"Did you hear me?"

"Yes," she whispered, "but couldn't you just confess to one thing?"

Her words trembled. I looked up and down the hallway, searching for something to explain what was happening. "Listen, I really don't have anything to say to you, okay? Everything's going good right now." I checked for her feet under her door—they didn't move. "When I have something to spill, I promise I'll come back."

The piano scales sounded eerie against her silence, and then her crying. Her weeping was a rusty swing set creaking in the wind. I didn't have time for this. I barely understood my own grief. I grabbed the rosary, slipped it in my pocket along with the flyer. My skirt sagged a little.

"I'll come back another time," I said, almost as a promise, and inched away. I considered whether skipping out on a crying nun was a sin and whether that was worse than stealing her rosary. At the first-floor landing, I decided that stealing was definitely worse. Before I opened the door to leave the building, I thought I could hear her asking if I was still there, but maybe my guilt had imagined her voice. The whole building smelled of burned popcorn. I needed a hit. It was time to go home.

Home was an abandoned apartment I shared with roughly twenty people. Except for my Audrey Hepburn poster hanging by two nails, the space was pretty empty. A couch with no cushions sat opposite the front door, and the rest of the living room writhed with rows of sleeping bodies. It was past midnight. The traffic light outside our window tinted the room in red, green, and then yellow. I'd shot up in the ferry bathroom and had already spent a few hours sleeping on the deck, dreaming that a man was rubbing my back and telling me not to worry about things like sins or sacrifice. The kitchen light was on and below the light was Jonesy, asleep, his limbs and clumpy hair splattered all over our futon. I took off my sneakers and squeezed my feet between sleeping thighs, ears, and elbows and made my way diagonally.

We all took turns sleeping on the futon. That night, while I wiped down my sample case in the kitchen sink, Jonesy woke up, tapped the futon, and told me it was okay for me to sleep with him. He said this in a way that made me think I had once asked him for permission.

"If I sleep with you tonight, does that mean I'll lose my turn when it comes up?"

"Yup!" Wimpy shouted from the bathroom.

I told Jonesy thanks but no thanks, that I'd rather stick it out.

"Suit yourself."

"Okay," I said.

"You always do."

I didn't know what he meant by this—I'd only been living there a week, maybe ten days. "What's that supposed to mean?"

"Nothing." He shook out his sleeping bag, sending to the linoleum a spent syringe and a bag of Chips Ahoy.

"No, really. Tell me."

"Well, since you ask." He found the pipe he was looking for. "We think you're sort of selfish." He lit up, took a hit, and exhaled long enough for me to feel envy. "You see, the girls here share themselves, but not you. You think you're too *good* for—"

"I'm pregnant," I said, surprising myself. I'd never said the word out loud.

"Shit." He took another big drag and slapped his forehead. "Am I the father?"

"No."

"You sure?"

"We've never had sex," I said.

"Thank. Fucking. God."

Jonesy was an okay guy. He sold stolen bicycles but never stole them himself. He said he was too out of shape for that kind of work even though he was tall and thin and looked healthy enough.

"Pregnant!" Wimpy bolted from the bathroom, holding the water bucket we used to flush the toilet. "Oh, for fuck sake, big congrats to ya!"

Wimpy was from England and smoked a lot of meth. I almost said thanks.

"I'm not keeping it," I told her.

"What! Why the fuck not!"

"Because I'm sixteen."

"So? We were all young once. And you'd make a great mum."

I thought about my own mother. "I don't think so," I said. "And plus, I don't have any money."

"But you have us!"

"You have less money."

"I'm just trying to help. You don't have to be nasty about it." She marched off and sulked at the other end of the kitchen counter. She was the toughest girl I knew and also the most sensitive. One time I overheard a guy asking her why she was called Wimpy. She punched him in the gut and said, "Because I'm not."

I walked up to her. "I'm sorry, Wimp. I can't seem to do anything right today."

"That's fine." She fired up the little burner someone had made out of two soda can bottoms. "I'm not hurt. I'm used to people's nastiness." She opened a tub of Spam, slid the pink block onto the counter, and scraped off the gelatin using her fingernails. With a bobby pin she found in her hair, she sliced the meat into three thick hunks.

"You want one?"

I shook my head.

She skewered a slab with the prongs of her pin and grilled it over the flame. The oily coating sparked.

"Hey, Wimp?"

"Yup."

"You ever been pregnant?"

"Millions of times. It's beautiful, that feeling, you know? I'd bite my entire arm off to be knocked up again."

"Wow. The entire arm. I really didn't expect you to say that."

"Oh sure. There's nothing like having an amphibian inside your body."

"Or that."

"Just think about it! It can live underwater! It's like a reptile." She turned over the meat. "That's what I wanted to study when I was a nipper. Turtles and alligators and reptiles. What is that, a terpetologist? A perpetologist? Whatever the name, that's what I wanted to be. Why you nattering on about reptiles anyway?"

I told her that I wasn't.

"Then why so many bloody questions about them then?"

"But...I only asked because...because I'm pregnant."

"Pregnant! I ruddy well better congratulate ya then, shouldn't I?" She put the meat down to give me a hug.

"Hey, Wimp?"

"Yeah?"

"How many bags you smoke today?"

"You reckon it's a boy or a girl? If it's a girl, let's name her Pippa. I always wanted to name a girl Pippa because—"

"I'm *not* having it," I said, maybe too harshly.

She touched my hand and whispered, "Why the fuck not?"

"Wimpy?"

"Yeah?"

"We just talked about this, like five seconds ago."

"What? You winding me up?" She took her skewer off the fire and nibbled. "Well, was I funny at least?"

"Hilarious." Suddenly I felt tired—tired enough to consider Jonesy's futon offer. He was already passed out, though.

"You going to have it then?" Wimpy asked, and I grabbed her shoulders. "I am *not* going to have it. I don't want it. Don't you understand? It's impossible for me to have it." I hadn't realized I was shaking her. It felt good and I couldn't stop. She was light, like an old paper doll.

"My...Spam...needs...me," she said, and I finally let go. She looked confused. Like a kid waiting in the rain for a school bus that wasn't coming. She nibbled at her dinner without saying another word, and I trudged into the bathroom, knowing I had hurt her feelings. With the door closed, I took off my blouse and hung it on a clothesline we had tied to two exposed pipes in the wall. I hung my skirt, too, with the rosary still in it. The tub was dry and peeling. I stepped into it and lay there awhile, touching my belly, the start of a swell, wondering if the baby could sense my father's temper and my mother's insanity through my hands.

As soon as I fell into the silence, Wimpy barged in and told me about the bleach.

"See? The stain just disappears!" she said, her body unable to contain her excitement as she poured bleach onto an old rag.

"I'm not so sure about this, Wimp."

"No, no, no, it's really easy. All we have to do is saturate the tampon." She fished a plastic cup from the trash, dumped out the sludge that was in there into the sink, poured in the bleach, and held the tampon by the string, dipping it into the cup like a teabag. "Then you put it way up in there, deeper than normal."

"That sounds like it's gonna hurt. Does it hurt?"

"How the fuck should I know? Now, you ready to crack-on or not?"

"Who taught you this?"

"People do it all the time," she said, and handed me the cup.

"And it works?"

"I don't look like a doctor, now do I? It works or it doesn't, that's the best I can do."

"It smells awful."

"Here I am trying to help you snuff that little bugger and all you do is complain." She turned her back to me, shaking her head.

I apologized but she wouldn't face me.

"I'm not upset," she said, picking at a wad of gum stuck to her foot. "It just hurts when people don't believe the things I say."

I again told her I was sorry. "I wasn't sure at first, but I trust you. You know lots of things," I said. "I'll do it now. I promise."

"Really?" She finally turned around. "Okay. I'll be right out here if you need me," she said, leaving the bathroom.

"Hey, Wimp?" I stopped the door from closing.

She cupped my face with both hands. "Yeah?"

"You ever been to confession?"

"Fuck no," she said, and gave me a tiny slap. "Love means never having to say you're sorry. Remember that."

After she left I sat on the toilet and tried to understand what she could've meant. I had no idea. The cup stared at me from the edge of the sink, and I thought about the baby and tried to picture me as its mother. I wondered what my own mother would think of me being pregnant. She'd dig in there and kill the baby herself. Kill it with her own bare hands while crying to God.

I grabbed my sneakers, shoved the tampon deep into the left one, and then put them both on. The cold wetness stung my toes. I'd go for a walk and toss it in the trash.

When I came out of the bathroom Wimpy looked at me with teary eyes and hugged me with a lot of feeling. "I'm so sorry you had to go through that," she said.

First, I went to a hospital.

In the crowded emergency room, a nurse behind the counter told me they didn't perform that sort of thing there, that I should go to a clinic. Then she asked me to step aside since I didn't really have an emergency. "Tell that to my stomach," I told her. She said that wasn't where the baby was.

Then I went to a clinic.

The sun felt cold, and I was proud of myself for having shot up exactly the right amount. Just enough to see the world without being in it. Everything—the cars and buses and curses from cabbies, the bodies that rushed by, as well as the ones that surrounded me like zombies— appeared beautiful and cinematic in my private view- finder. "God loves you. This is from God," a woman whispered right in my ear, holding out an egg. She clung to my arm. Her hair smelled of wood polish. We were in the middle of the sidewalk, in front of the clinic, and the woman had silver hair and blue discs for eyes. "I really love you," I told her, and was certain that that was the right answer. I walked past her, and now a boy came forward, a blond one, wearing a keyboard necktie. "God loves you. This is from God," he said. I fingered his tie like I was playing a song and moved past him, almost running over a girl who came up to my waist. She was maybe five years old. "God told me you can have this," the girl said, smiling, offering her gift with both hands. I took the egg. It was hardboiled. The sky was blue and had been swept clean of clouds. I wondered if it was Easter. I thanked the girl, put the egg in my jacket pocket, and walked into the clinic.

In the waiting room, I came down enough to understand that it was not Easter and the egg people were protesters of some kind. Some guy wearing a tool belt was duct-taping the front door glass with cardboard. All the windows facing the street were shut. The blinds were shut. Once in a while I peeked outside. The protestors had a tall wastebasket filled with eggs. They handed them out to everyone on the street, except the homeless.

I sat across from a TV and my eyes throbbed too much, trying to follow all the magic in *I Dream of Jeannie*. Jeannie was too happy. Who was she trying to fool? She was crossing her arms and blinking, making a puppy appear and disappear, over and over again, right when a black girl with tight shorts and loopy earrings walked in front of the television set and slipped into the bathroom. The sign above the TV read: NO FOOD. NO DRINK. NO RADIO. It said nothing about shooting up in the bathroom. I'd been waiting for too long and now I was coming down fast. I needed to be high for the abortion. Somebody had given me that advice but I couldn't remember who. Was it the nun? Had I told her about the baby? I imagined the bathroom sink, sparkling clean with a wide counter and maybe a lounge chair, and the more I thought about it, the more my arm started to heat up. I flexed my hand, waited, tapped the gear in my jacket pocket to make sure it was there. I took the egg out, rolled it like dough between my palms while hoping for the black girl to exit the bathroom any second. She was taking too long. I couldn't focus on the TV anymore or on anything but an itch that burned my arm. I counted, made predictions that the girl would come out by ten, and then twenty.

On twenty-three, a redheaded girl in a lab coat burst into the waiting area and called out "Suzy." Her voice was too loud for the size of the room. I hated her instantly, ignored her as best as I could and went back to my counting. She wouldn't shut up, though—she called the name again. There was a couple holding hands in the corner, two white girls with headphones next to the brochure rack, and three Puerto Rican girls by the water fountain.

"Suzy?" This time the girl said it looking right at me. "Suzy Q. Wong?"

I jumped up. That was the name I'd put on my forms.

The redhead took me through a door, down a hallway, and into a small green room decorated with posters of our insides. She sat with a folder on her lap. I sat facing her.

"So. Your test came back positive. You are definitely pregnant."

"What test?"

"You gave us a urine sample, remember?"

"Yes," I said, trying to remember.

She clicked her pen into action. "And now I see that you're looking to get some information about an abortion?"

"Actually, I just want one, if that's okay." I tried a smile.

"Well, it's not that simple." She pushed her glasses up her freckled nose. "I have to ask you some questions."

I told myself to sit still. "Okay."

"First off, when was your last period? You left that blank."

It seemed like years ago. I told her I wasn't sure.

She held up a calendar, flipped back a month, and another, and I still couldn't remember.

"Were you using protection?"

"Sure."

"Is that a yes or no?"

"Yes, uh, could I use the bathroom?" I couldn't breathe.

"This won't take long. Let's just get through it, okay?" She turned to a new page in the folder. "Now, do you have insurance?"

"Insurance?" I crossed my legs and kicked her shoe by accident.

"Yes. You checked the box." She showed me the square with my X.

"I'm sorry, I don't have it," I said.

She made a big deal out of scratching out my mistake and circling the no box. "Are you working currently?"

I nodded. I felt good about finally having the right answer. "I sell Avon," I managed to say. "It's a pretty good gig. There's no interview. You just mail them money and they send you samples."

"That's nice," the girl said.

I wiped my nose on my sleeve. She handed me a Kleenex. "I can work whenever I want and the money's pretty good."

"And how much would you say you make in a month?"

I had no idea. I couldn't think about numbers. "A few

thousand, I guess. Easy." I liked how I sounded. Honest, confident, sturdy. "You could, too, if you want. I could show you how."

She scribbled something, smiling at my folder, and pulled out a calculator. Without a word, she punched in numbers and the crunching of the keys made me grind my teeth, the sound reminding me of a place I couldn't name. "Your sliding scale co-pay," the girl said, "is two hundred dollars. Can you pay any portion of that today?"

I studied the calculator, her crossed knees, the tip of her shoe bouncing impatiently. "I thought this was a free clinic."

"It is and it isn't. It's pay-what-you-can. The two hundred is based on your salary scale. Unless . . ."

"Unless what?"

"Unless you weren't being honest about your employment. I'd understand if you—"

I shot up from my seat. "I'm honest. What, you don't believe me?"

"That's not what I'm saying, I'm trying to help you."

"I thought this was a free clinic, that's all." Standing up quickly had been a bad idea. I zeroed in on her hand, her thumb slowly unclicking her pen. "I have to think about it," I told her, and tried to find the door. "It's not the money. I just, you know, have to think about the whole thing."

"I understand," she said, but if she had really understood she would've taken me in her arms, mopped the sweat off my face, and told me I didn't have to try anymore, that I wasn't alone, that I could just lie down and be saved.

"You go ahead and think about it," she said, closing my folder. "You can always come back, as long as it's not too late."

I thanked her but wanted to spit in her eyes.

I went back to the building where the nun lady lived.

"Forgive me, Sister, for it has been never since my last confession."

A song from *The Sound of Music* seeped into the hallway. I flipped my notepad to a page where I'd jotted down all my sins I could think of.

"You still there?"

"I am right by your side," she said.

"Okay. I just want to start off by saying that I've done some bad things in my life but I haven't killed anyone."

"Of course not. You're too good of a soul to do such a thing."

"I've done little things, like..." I looked at my list again. "Okay, a while ago, I lifted a soundtrack to *Fame*. But I'm going to cut that out."

"You wanted music. Who could punish you for that?"

This was going good. "Okay, and yesterday, I saw this dead bird in the park. I wanted to give it a good burial but I was too scared to touch it. I should've done it, though. I've been feeling bad about it since. I mean, nobody deserves to go like that. Everyone should die with respect, right? Even the fuckups. Because you never know, they might've done one really good thing, and just because they turn out stupid or rotten doesn't mean they're bad, through and through, right? Everybody deserves to die with respect."

"Absolutely," she said.

I leaned against the doorjamb. "I guess I sometimes wonder how I'm gonna go. I'd probably want to go in my sleep, like Bruce Lee or Marilyn Monroe."

"Yes, she was beautiful, wasn't she?"

"I won't lie. I've thought about killing myself. But I'd never do it because no one would care. But then that's what makes me want to do it in the first place."

"One of life's many ironies."

"And I guess I should come clean and tell you that I shoot up sometimes."

"With guns?"

"No, like heroin. I shoot it into my arm."

"That can't be good."

"Sometimes my hand. Anyway...what I'm trying to say is that it's nothing to worry about. I'm not addicted, like the people I live with. I have a job. I sell Avon. I got things under control. Except..." I leaned in closer. "I took one of those pregnancy tests, and it gave me a plus sign. And now I'm all turned around. I mean, I can't have a baby now, right? I feel like I'm onto something with this Avon thing." I paused there to give her a chance to speak. She didn't say a word. Not even a sigh.

"I don't even know how I can get the"—I couldn't say the word—"to get it taken care of but, I was wondering, if I do it, if I get it taken care of, can I get...pre-forgiven?"

"What do you mean?"

"You forgive people *after* they do bad stuff but can I get forgiven before?"

"Well," she said, stretching the word. "I'm going to need a minute to think about that one."

I looked to the floor. Her silence made me bite my

nails, then the calluses around my nails, and the longer I waited for her to say something, the more I hated the way I'd sounded. Too desperate. Too needy. I decided to end on a different note and added that I felt guilty for being scared of dwarves with their short arms. "Okay, that's everything," I said, and waited again. Without making a drop of noise I put my ear flat against the wood and concentrated. A muffled voice in the background, maybe from a radio or a TV. I crouched down to look for her pink fuzzy slippers, or any sign of her, when a woman, wearing a pantsuit, marched up the hallway stairs.

"Can I help you?" she asked, pushing up her sleeves. Behind her was a man carrying a large ring of keys.

I got up off the floor. "No, I was just . . ."

The woman stepped in front of me and rattled the doorknob. "Mom, you have to open up, okay?"

"Who're you supposed to be?" the man asked, eyeing my sample case. "You read the sign out there? 'No solicitors' means 'No solicitors.'"

"I'm not selling anything."

"I have the super here, Mom, and he's going to let me in."

"Oh, Susan," the nun lady said. "That's really kind of you, but really, I'm just fine. You don't have to come in."

"This look like any of your business?" the super asked me, and I sidestepped toward the stairs as he tried out a few keys. Pretty soon he was turning the knob.

"Please, Susan, you can't," the nun lady begged. The daughter entered anyway, swinging the door wide, giving me a glimpse of the nun's balding carpet and a framed macramé hooked to the wall. It was of purple flowers, the words *Love grows here* hovering over them. I pulled the rosary from my pocket and flung it at the daughter. It bounced off the door frame instead, making the super turn around and hate me more. Before he could get a word in, I ran down the stairs and out of the building.

Oh, please let's have the baby, Wimpy whined. *Think of all the things we can steal if we had a baby with us. No cop's gonna nab a girl with a baby. A baby gets smiles. The baby's our shield. It'll protect us from evil. The baby's our answer. Baby! Baby! Baby!*

I knocked on a door. Who knew where or when this was. I blinked my eyes and suddenly I was here, and then not here. There, and then not there. Time flew, my body shrank, my stomach grew to the size of a teakettle, and

I kept on working even though nobody answered their door anymore. Except this guy.

"Yeah?"

He stood in front of me wearing a white tank top that showcased his tattooed arms but made his chest look like a stick of gum.

"Hi. I'm the Avon Lady and—"

"Fuck. Really? Shit." He rubbed the back of his neck and said, "Get in here," pulling me in.

The long hallway led us to a living room.

"Sit down." He pointed to a couch. "You want something to drink?"

I told him I did.

"We got vodka, tequila, beer. I'm gonna light up. You want some pot?"

I'd shoved off earlier and was coming down, so I said yes, without sounding too desperate. He disappeared into the kitchen, where stacks of albums and eight-tracks crowded the counter.

When he came back, he dropped me a beer and gently lowered himself down on a rocking chair that was cushioned with an inflatable doughnut. After letting out a short breath, he gingerly placed his feet up on the coffee table, one foot at a time. Black military boots, laces tied tight. Hanging on the wall behind him was a humongous poster of kittens—tiny puffs of silver felines clawing at a dangling ball of yarn. Next to that, a picture of a spring garden. The place could've been decorated by a ten-year-old girl. Everything in the room went against him—the unicorn stickers on windows clashed with his skull tattoos, the ballet figurines didn't go with the scar across his collarbone, and the fat, stuffed panda sitting next to me didn't explain his pencil-thin mustache. He was more black than white, giving him a golden smooth face and a reddish Afro.

He packed his pipe and lit up. "My wife's coming out in a sec," he said, holding in his hit. "You got makeup in that thing, right?"

I told him I did and peeled back the tab on my beer.

"Can I see?" he asked, passing me the pipe.

"Sure." First, I took a good hit. I liked him. He was already a great customer. After my second toke, I opened my sample case.

"Yeah, my wife, she don't usually wear makeup, but..." He pointed to the bottles. "What's in there?"

"Foundation."

"What does it do?"

"It covers up blemishes and zits and smoothes out your face." My eyelashes felt heavy. The pot was working fast. "I think it's nice you're getting makeup for your wife," I said, and I sort of meant it.

"Yeah, well, a little while back, I fell off a ladder," he said, leaning back on his chair. "And this huge branch, as long as my arm, just shot up my ass."

I nodded, trying to act like I understood what he'd just said. I wasn't sure how the branch had anything to do with his wife but I listened as he went on to tell me things I didn't care to know.

"The branch just skewered me clean. It missed all the important stuff, and stopped just two centimeters from my heart. The doctors sliced me up pretty good, from the neck down. Lifted up my rib cage like it was the hood of a car and hacksawed the branch into three parts. Pulled each piece out. Then they rinsed me clean. Poured buckets of water in me and sucked out all the wood chips."

I didn't know what my face looked like but the guy nodded and said, "Yeah. Tell me about it. I got photos if you wanna see."

The pot had punched me between the eyes. I couldn't tell if it was my turn to speak. "I should get going," I said, trying to get up.

"Wait. Why're you leaving?"

"Because you just told me something really crazy and I don't know what to do with the feeling."

He pointed to the pipe in my hand.

"Good point," I said, and sat back down. I took another drag, a strong one. "Did it hurt?"

"The operation?"

"No. The tree."

"I couldn't even scream it hurt so much. I had to whisper for help. I was up there, like, thirty minutes."

My head was heavy and light, an empty cookie jar. I passed the pipe back. "That's a long time with a tree inside you."

"Gave me time to think." He blew into the pipe until it whistled and then refilled it. "I thought a lot about pain. I have never been that focused in my life. Here," he said, and gave back the pipe.

"Are you okay now?" I tried not to look at his midsection.

"I'm okay. I guess I'm still a little pissed," he said, shaking his head.

I took a drag and held it. "Jesus, I'd be pissed, too."

"What? Why would Jesus be pissed?"

I freed the smoke. "I'm sorry. I don't know what I'm

saying. I'm just talking, that's all." I passed the pipe again, this time turning it so he could grab it by the handle.

"I'm pissed at my wife." He took a long look at the door behind him.

"What did she do?"

"She used to be a cashier."

"No, I mean…" I could feel the giggles rising. "What did she do to piss you off?"

"Oh, that. She had an affair."

"Okay," I said, telling myself not to laugh because affairs weren't funny.

"With my brother. She was screwing him. In our bed."

I pinched the side of my thigh to stop the giggles, dug my nails so deep until my eyes filled with pain and sympathy. This was good pot. This was a good guy. He deserved better.

"We were living in a house in Jersey. I went up the ladder to scare the shit out of them from the window and what do I do. I almost get killed."

The ceiling looked like icing, with too many nooks and crannies. "I bet you really freaked them out, though. Seeing someone with a branch in his body is pretty scary," I said, feeling wise and old.

"Yeah, well." He glanced at the door again. "She didn't look all that frightened."

"Trust me, she was, on the inside." I grabbed the stuffed panda beside me and sniffed it. It smelled like fabric softener.

"Maybe." The guy inhaled enough to make him cough. The smoke fogged his face.

"Your brother, too. He probably ran out of the house, like a little mouse."

"I don't think so," he said, clearing his throat. "He took his time getting dressed. I looked up and saw him at the window, putting on his tie, looking down at me, a fucking shish kebab."

I hugged the panda.

"He was smoking a cigarette. Probably one of mine."

I sat up on the edge of the couch and stopped the urge to touch him on his shoulder. "That's really wrong," I said. "You didn't deserve that."

Right then a small pregnant girl came out wearing business clothes—a jacket, a blouse, a tent of skirt covering her enormous belly, and high heels that made her teeter. Her right eye was half-closed and bloodshot, and below it, on her cheek, was a huge bruise the size of a fist.

"Hi," she said, her voice sounding like soft bread.

The guy got up quickly and hung his thick arm over her shoulders. "She just got called in for a job interview. Maybe you got something to cover up the..."

"Right," I said. "Right."

He gave her a smile and the girl tried to give one back but the swelling wouldn't bend.

I put the panda down and gathered my samples. "The light. It's probably better in the bathroom," I said quietly, as if lowering my voice would make the bruise hurt less. She went in first and I followed her, passing the guy without looking at him once.

The light in the bathroom was a dirty orange and made everything—the towels, the Minnie Mouse shower curtain, the rubber ducky on the sink—seem rusted. The girl stood with her hands resting on the roof of her belly, looking at herself in the cabinet mirror with eyes deader than stones. It scared me to see her that big and that sad. On the toilet seat I set my case down, opened it up with a little trouble, reorganized the tiny bottles of foundation alphabetically and then by light to dark, as if it mattered. I imagined my stomach as big as hers while fumbling to open each sampler, trying to decide what shade to apply. I'd never cared before.

"Baja Summer," I whispered, and showed her the bottle before gently dabbing her cheekbone with a triangle sponge. Up close the bruise looked to be rotting. My hands shook. I asked her if it hurt but she said nothing. She was unreachable. She didn't even wince. She just stared into those eyes of hers while I caked on layers of new skin.

"It's not what you think," she said at some point.

"I'm not thinking anything."

"Sure you are. You think you know something about me."

"I'm just concentrating."

"And him."

I poured more cream onto the sponge, taking more time than usual. "I know he's the one doing the punching," I said, finally.

"Like I said. You don't know anything."

"Fine. I don't know anything."

"You're stupid, just like the rest of them."

"Look," I said calmly but could feel my throat knotting up. "I don't know who or what you're talking about but I'm not *that* stupid. I've done a lot of stupid things, and everything's really fucked up right now, but that does not mean that he isn't the one doing the punching, okay? Nothing you say can stop me from knowing that."

"You don't get it."

"You're right. I don't." I threw my sponge into the sink and started packing. "And you know what, I don't give a shit."

"We tried everything," she said.

"Well, I've tried everything, too, and I'm tired of trying."

"Knitting needles, clothes hangers. He's even kicked me in the stomach."

I shut my sample case. I couldn't listen.

"It's so big now," she said. "It's a big fat baby that won't go away. Can you believe that?" The words popped out of her mouth. I wanted to tape her lips shut or rip my ears off.

"You girls doing okay in there?" the guy called from the living room.

She studied her face in the mirror. "You put too much on. I look like I'm melting."

I grabbed my case. I needed out.

"He wasn't trying to hurt me," she said, putting a hand on my arm. "He just wanted to kill the baby. But it refuses to die." She let go and grabbed some tissue. "Isn't that the funniest thing you've ever heard?" she asked, dabbing her nose, letting out either a laugh or a cry, I couldn't tell.

I suppose that was where I'd gotten the idea.

That I should kill the baby before it got too big. Before it killed me. The fact that I could die while trying didn't really factor into the decision. I shot up in the ferry bathroom that night. The need wasn't something I could reason with, and I used up more than I should have, leaving me dry for the next day. But it was a good hit, nothing to be ashamed of.

Afterward, I climbed the stairs to the upper deck, felt my way outside, and lay down on a bench so orange I wanted to drink it. The stars were out—all that silver, squinting in the dark, knowing exactly who they were and where their place was in the night. The regulars surrounded me, smoking, sipping, bobbing their heads to a guy playing guitar. I shut my eyes and saw the baby floating in my belly, just like the one I'd seen in a jar in sixth grade. It can breathe underwater, I thought, like some salamander. Wimpy was right after all. *And it's breakin' my heart you're leavin'—baby I'm grievin'.* They all sang while the little one started crawling up and down my chest and stomach, her nails scraping my ribs in a way I didn't like. *Ooh, baby baby it's a wild world* ... I rubbed my belly to find her, and then I punched her and punched again. She wouldn't stop moving, so I kept hitting, with both fists, harder and harder, to the beat of the song.

"Hey, you all right?"

I snapped open my eyes. There was a hand on my shoulder and the hand belonged to a man sitting next to me. "I haven't seen my mother in a long time," I heard myself say. His face reminded me of a cat I'd found in the trash once.

"None of us have," he said, passing me a bottle.

I took a pull so long the man snatched the pint back, pushed me away before scooting to the other end of the bench. I apologized. I told him my dog had just died. It just came out that way. I couldn't have people knowing things about me but I wanted the right to be sad. The man didn't hear or didn't care. Neither did the bearded guy across from us. He'd stopped playing guitar to have a drink himself, and the cigarette he kept trapped between the strings went on smoking all by itself.

I walked to the railing, stepped up onto the middle rung, and leaned over the edge, looking straight down at the white water ribbons the ferry left behind. The engine revved and the wind sprayed water onto my face and neck. I felt cleaner than I'd felt in a long time. The river was going to rinse my baby away. Rinse the baby and make me simple again.

Falling was easy.

When I hit the water, I did not hold my breath. I didn't move and I wasn't afraid. Opening my eyes and opening my mouth, I drank through every part of my body, wanting to stay down for as long as possible. I thought of the baby inside me, and me inside my mother, as the string of water ran between my ears, behind my eyes, and inside my heart and lungs. This is what it feels like to be filled with love, I thought. Pure, meaningless love.

Did I do right? I asked.

Absolutely, she said. You gave your true self to God and He gave His true answer. Needles spiked my arm. A scratchy blanket covered me from the breast down. Stiff, plastic tubes sprayed cold air up my nose, drying out the back of my mouth. I woke up in a hospital room that smelled of pennies. I was cold. I was beeping. The baby was dead but they couldn't see. The doctor, the nurse, the policeman all had enormous eyes but they couldn't see. Leaning too close over my face, all they did was ask stupid questions. *You fall in or did you mean to do it? Is there anyone we can call? Can you tell us your name? What's your name?*

I closed my eyes and sang, I'm fine, I'm fine, I'm fine.

Frank

The meeting was held in an elementary school, in a class-room with a snake tank and green penmanship placards above a blackboard. I sat in the back row, on a foldout chair under a hanging globe, and listened to a mustached man share how he'd been introduced to heroin during a tour in Vietnam. After him was a stockbroker who'd traded his wife and kids for his love of crack, followed by a stage actor who was handed the worst role of his life—as a crystal meth junkie.

"Such bullshit," someone whispered.

Three empty seats to my left, a guy sat hunched for-ward with elbows on knees, shaking his head.

"Absolute bullshit," he said again, and I was sure that this time he'd said it for my benefit.

Frank

"What?" I whispered back.

He slid over to the seat next to me and spoke louder even though we were now much closer. "How come everybody was a fucking hero before they found crank? How come every asshole who goes up there had a shitload of money, a perfect job and a perfect wife and a two-car garage before he lost it all to base?" He moved his hands too much when he talked, and I thought he might smack me by accident. "Sacks of dog shit. Just once I want somebody to go up there and say, hey, you know what? I was a fucking asshole before I slammed shit up my arms, and guess what, I'm still a fucking asshole."

A few heads turned to judge us.

"I'm Frank, by the way." He leaned back, stretched his legs, and spread his arm across the back of my chair. "I'm an addict and an alcoholic."

During break, Frank and I smoked outside in the schoolyard, by the jungle gym, away from the others. From there, we could see the double doors that opened to the yard, the hallway, the people congregating by the refreshment table. The sun was falling, giving its last bit of life to the telephone wires above us.

"So, what's your poison?" Frank asked, lighting up two cigarettes.

"Heroin mostly, and some other stuff."

"Wanna know mine?" He passed me a smoke. "Sobriety. It's fucking killing me. I can't take all the bullshit. They got it backwards. All these con artists." He flapped a hand toward the school. "When I was high, that was the real me."

Everything about Frank moved too much. His eyes, the size of gumballs, rattled when he talked. His right hand shuttled his cigarette to and from his mouth, while the left kept scrubbing the top of his thinning scalp. He paced. He spat. He shifted his weight, sometimes perching a foot on the jungle gym railing, sometimes rocking side to side, with his arms crossed. He was the opposite of me. I could hardly move. All I wanted was to unfeel and unthink, a phase my counselor hoped I'd get past.

"Four hundred and sixty-two days," Frank blurted, tapping the breast pocket of his black leather jacket.

It took me a second to figure out he was tapping his sobriety chip. "That's a lot of days," I said.

"Means nothing. That's just how long I've been fooling myself. I still got some drinking left in me. Drinking, fucking, snorting, smoking—all that. I know it, they know it. Shit, even you probably know it."

I smiled. "If you say so."

"How about you. You think you're done?"

I glanced at the back of my hand, the tiny scab above my ring finger, and told him I was.

Frank threw his head back and laughed, the cave of his mouth stretching wide before shrinking into coughs. When he finally calmed down, he rubbed his chest and said, "Trust me, sweetheart, you're not even close to being done."

"Thank God," I said, which sent him rolling again. I laughed, too, and tried to calculate how much of my response was based on truth. I didn't mind Frank's prediction of my failure. The people at the hospital clinic—my counselor, the nurses, the social workers— showed too much hope for me. It was in the way they smiled when watching me swallow my cup of pills, the way they spoke softly when I showed even a grain of emotion. I didn't know what to do with all their hope. It surrounded my head. It sealed my face and suffocated. Hope was based on the unknown, and I liked knowing things. Like that I was going to fail. Failure had better odds. You could depend on it. So when Frank said with absolute certainty that I had more using left in me, I couldn't help but feel relieved. Maybe even happy.

By the middle of his second cigarette he told me how he'd dropped out of night school to work as a mechanic but somehow ended up in jail for destruction of personal property.

"It started with a chicken suit," he said.

"You destroyed a chicken suit?"

"No. I *bought* a chicken suit. And I put it on because I was trying to win back a girl."

"In a chicken suit."

"You wanna tell the story?" he asked, his hand gesturing to an invisible microphone between us. He was angry. His voice got louder, his eyes bulged, and his veins made a tree on his neck, but his anger didn't frighten me like my father's. I told him I was sorry and asked him to go on.

"It's okay, I just have to tell it all at once or the story gets messed up."

"Okay."

"Okay. So I put on this thing and drive half an hour to get to this girl's apartment. It's like midnight, and she's not there, so I grab her spare key from under her mat and let myself in."

"Did anyone see you?"

"Like who?"

"Never mind," I said. "I thought maybe a neighbor might've seen you."

"How the fuck should I know? Nobody saw nothing, okay?"

"I'm sorry."

"Jesus, will you stop apologizing? Just let me tell the story, okay?"

"You're right," I said, and could feel myself slipping back into a familiar role—listening to others, swirling in their stories, touching and breathing in their lives so I didn't have to be in mine. At least, that was what my counselor had told me.

"Anyway. Like I was saying, I go into her place, and right away I see she's living with some fucker. There's two toothbrushes, two bathrobes, and his is made of velvet. I mean, who the fuck does he think he is, Telly Savalas?"

"Velvet's kind of creepy," I said, to show I was on his side.

"So I get depressed, seeing all his shit there, and I just start raiding their cabinets looking for booze. This was my fifth time falling off the wagon and I start drinking everything—rum, peach schnapps, sambuca, Grand Marnier, whatever—and I'm getting really fucked up. Then, all of a sudden, I gotta take a piss."

"It makes sense."

"But I'm in the chicken suit. And I can't reach the zipper—my neighbor had to zip me up, remember?"

He hadn't mentioned that part but I let it go.

"I gotta take a leak so bad but I don't wanna piss all over myself, so I grab a knife from the kitchen and cut a hole in the costume, near my dick. And I'm slicing and slicing and the piss is about to come up my throat it's so bad. By the time I get my dick out, I just start pissing all over the kitchen floor."

I made a face but Frank didn't see because all he saw was the inside of his story.

"And it feels so good. Then I start thinking, hey, maybe it feels good because I'm pissing on *their* linoleum. So I walk over to the couch."

"No."

"You got it. All over their couch, their pillows, their fucking bathroom mat, their hand towels. When I run out of piss, I drink more and wait and piss all over his business suits, their bed. I even piss into her shampoo bottle."

"Now, that's going too far," I half-joked, but Frank said, "Yeah, maybe," and considered it seriously.

"Anyway, after all that, I need a smoke, so I go out to the backyard."

"Why didn't you just smoke in the apartment?"

"Josie hated the smell of cigarettes. I didn't wanna be rude. Plus, I was burning up in that getup. I needed some air. So I'm sitting in her backyard, on this picnic table she shares with some neighbor upstairs, and I'm smoking and drinking, and who knows what fucked-up things are going on in my head, but I start thinking that the neighbor's porch light is bugging the shit out of me. It's so damn bright."

"Lightbulbs are funny that way."

"So I climb the neighbor's back porch stairs, and the wood, it creaks like some animal. But I get to the landing and I unscrew the lightbulb." Frank fired up another cigarette and pushed the smoke out his nose. "Five minutes later, the cops are slamming my face on the grass and trying to cuff my chicken wrists."

"You got arrested for unscrewing a lightbulb?"

"Think about it," he said, tapping his temple. "You're a

girl and you're sleeping alone. You hear somebody climbing up your stairs and so you get up, you go to the kitchen, and all you see out your back porch door is a shadow of a giant bird, reaching up and unscrewing your fucking lightbulb." He cleared his throat and spit. "God, that poor woman. She must've lost her throat screaming."

"What about your girl?"

"She told the cops everything. About all the piss. She thought having the entire neighborhood watch me get arrested in a chicken suit wasn't embarrassing enough." Frank took a drag and the smoke scaled up his face and to the sky. It was dark now. Winter was coming. "I know what I did was really fucked up but I tell you what, I've never felt closer to the truth until that day. Whatever was flowing through my body that night—*that* was real. That anger was so fucking clean—I mean, when I was pissing all over their stuff, that was the single most honest moment I've ever lived in my life. That was me. The real me. My life right now, it's just all bullshit."

The meeting officers were herding people back into the classroom. Frank pitched his cigarette and headed in the opposite direction, toward the schoolyard gate. "C'mon, let's get the fuck outta here and get a drink."

Frank

His leaving surprised me. Sure, he had seemed frustrated, but I thought most of it was for show, as in, sobriety sucks but it's better than going to jail kind of thing. The ground felt suddenly uneven, as if the earth had tilted toward Frank, coaxing me to take that first step so the weight of my body and simple physics could make the decision for me. But I wasn't moving. I wondered if all that hospital hope had something to do with it. In any case, I didn't follow Frank, and it took a while for him to notice.

"I think I'm going to stick around," I whispered, but the sky was clear and my voice traveled far.

He slowed and then came to a stop. With hands shoved in his pockets, he kicked the toe of his sneaker into the pavement as if wanting to dig through. "They're trying to sell us a god that don't exist. You know that, right?"

"Yeah." I searched to say something really important but came up empty. "But I really like the sugar cookies."

"You gotta be fucking kidding me." He stared at the school entrance for a while as if its long hallway, now a fluorescent green, contained some dream he knew the ending of. "Fine," he said, finally, and stomped toward me. "Let's go hear some more bullshit so you can get your sugar cookies."

I gave him a little push and I could tell he liked it.

Right before we entered the classroom Frank asked if I had a sponsor.

I told him I didn't.

"Good," he said, patting me on my back. "I really wanna be there for you when you fall."

King's Manor

I sat on the park bench next to Ray, who was missing a leg. Winter was falling on us, on the shoulders of his faded army jacket, the metal rims of his wheelchair, the folded New York Yankees blanket covering his stump. Pushing his bare foot against the sidewalk, he rolled closer to the pigeons pecking at the snow. He couldn't wear shoes because his foot was too swollen, the skin around it tight and flaking. I wanted to slice it open for him, to let the pressure out. I wanted to free his veins.

I'd stopped shooting up and was working at a small nursing home. Except for my first name, I lied about everything on the job application. Nobody at work knew the real me, including Ray, the only person I ever talked to, though never about my past. He was a patient. He didn't have any family.

"You want one?" he asked, shaking his cigarette pack so a filter shot up. I took it. He caped a side of his jacket over his face to shield the flame from the wind. I lit mine off his. Most of his teeth were gone. When he took a drag, his lips curled into his mouth.

"They're cutting it off this week," he said, tossing crumbs to the birds by his foot.

I feigned ignorance, a new talent of mine.

He patted his good leg. "The blister's gone bad and the infection's spreading." He coughed and spat, turning his head away from me and the birds. "They're letting me keep the knee this time, though."

"That's good," I said. "Knees are good."

Somewhere far away a small dog was barking. Ray didn't blink. He let the tears fill his eyes. I wished he would cry, really loud, just so both of us could get past wondering whether he was going to or not.

"Now one's going to be shorter than the other." He wiped his nose on his wrist.

I wanted to tell him not to worry about that because his legs weren't the same length to begin with since one was a stump, but I couldn't think of a way to say it without sounding cruel or stupid.

"I still miss the other one. Ten years and it still itches sometimes."

"I know," I said.

"Is that so?" He glanced at me sideways, his sarcasm pinching the corners of his mouth.

"Where do you feel it?" I asked, feeling the need to make up for something.

He pointed his cigarette down at his invisible calf. "Drives me nuts. Can you imagine having an itch you can never scratch?"

I was about to say yes but thought better of it and told him no.

"Well, try. Just try and imagine it."

"Okay."

A little later I said, "Sometimes I feel an itch deep in my ears but I can't get to it."

He tossed his cigarette over the birds. "Yup," he said. "It's just like that, only now take away the head."

We sat in that Sunday quiet. Morning service would start soon. As an assistant to the activities coordinator, I was in charge of transporting patients into the chapel without incident. I told Ray we should get back.

"Just a little longer." He closed his eyes to the shredding sky, letting the snow make a veil of his face.

An orderly walking to work stopped to say hi. He said his name was Benny and that he was new. Ray stayed in his trance.

"Is he alive?" Benny asked, scrunching his brows. Benny had brown hair and cold, bluish skin, which made me think he should be wearing a hat and something thicker than his uniform scrubs. Stamped on the thigh of his pants was *King s Manor*—a tiny hole having eaten up the apostrophe. "Guess I'll see you in there," he said, hugging himself, giving me a smile that seemed too intimate. For years I would follow that smile without understanding what any of it meant, but I didn't know it then.

When Benny left, I turned to Ray. He still faced the sky, his eyes closed to the world. I crouched down and put his sock back on.

"Hey, Joon?"

"Yeah?"

He rolled up his bag of crumbs and tucked it inside his jacket. "Will you come to the hospital when they cut it off?"

A snow truck drove past, the noise of it silencing everything else. I told Ray I would go with him even though I knew I wouldn't. I prayed for him to hear the lie in my voice. Everything and everyone had to be thrown away—heroin dreams and alcohol and all the strays I'd met living as a runaway—so I could get a fresh start. And now I was clean but empty. I had nothing left to give. To Ray, or to anyone.

As I wheeled him back, he told me the date and time of the amputation, and I nodded, wondering what the doctors did with all those detached body parts.

That night I went home and put a plastic grocery bag over my head. I wanted to see what the head felt like, separate from my body. I cinched the bag tight around my neck and lay down without letting go of my grip. With my every breath the white plastic bag crinkled in and out, making too much noise, and the bare bulb hanging above me seemed foggy. My face turned damp. My breath smelled exactly like what I'd eaten for lunch—a bowl of instant noodles, a pickle. I tightened the grip on the bag, and eventually my breathing slowed, enough for me to sense a layer of mist licking my eyes. The plastic barely crinkled. Slowly my head began disremembering the body, sloughing it off gently, until all I could feel was my now-giant skull and my one arm, still strangling the bag. It was quiet. And then too quiet. That's when they came to me. My mother, Knowledge, Wink, Blue, and even my father. They all wedged their faces into the plastic bag, flattening my skin and folding my ears, and used up all the extra air to tell me that I deserved to be lonely, that I was selfish for having left them behind.

I snatched the bag off, gagging. I'd lasted about five minutes. After a rest, I tried again but didn't last as long. I felt dizzy. The back of my head tingled and sparked the proverbs my new sponsor had spoken. *Make amends to make progress. Repair the foundation and build a better life.* Frank's using again, my sponsor told me, biting into an empanada that stained his fingers. That man's running out of lives, he said.

When the pay phone rang it startled me. I slid out from my sleeping bag, walked to the other end of my studio, and stared at it, face-to-face, as it continued to ring. A leftover from when the place used to be a newsstand and candy store, the black phone was covered in OTB stickers and silver graffiti, except on the shiny metal faceplate that warped my nose. I didn't know its number, so I decided that the call couldn't be for me. After ringing sixteen more times, the person on the other end finally gave up.

The rings left an echo. It dawned on me then that people left echoes. Without thinking, I dropped two dimes and punched seven random buttons. No longer in service, the recording said. The White Pages, bound in a black binder, dangled below the phone. I opened to a page and picked a number without reading the name beside it.

"This better be Kilduff," a man said right away.

I hung up. I grabbed more dimes and called another number, and then another, feeling braver with each connection. I looked to see if my father was listed. He was. He picked up in three rings.

"Hello?" he answered in Korean. I breathed quietly, ran my finger over three initials carved on the side of the phone. "Hello," he said again, this time slower, as if he were scared of me.

I hung up.

His "hello" stayed with me for a while and faded, like the sunburned shapes behind closed eyes. And then I was alone again. I thought I could hear a hiss rising from my concrete floor. It was my sponsor again. *Being alone is like being with the last person you got high with. Get out of the house.*

Following his sound advice, I left my place and went to a neighborhood bar with a neon dartboard on the window. I drank shots of gin, the first taste of liquor in months, and the more I drank, the more I was convinced that alcohol was not the problem. By the third round, a guy came up and told me I was pretty. I'd seen him in the corner, playing darts by himself and taking breaks only to slip coins into the jukebox. He bought me Long Island iced teas and we talked about things like the crappy weather and drink prices being too high and how his wife had left him for their kid's karate instructor. He himself was a bagel maker. The secret ingredient, he said, was New York tap water. I told him that it didn't sound much like a secret, but by then our eyes were floating in alcohol and nothing mattered.

"You're lonely," I said, like a fact.

He waved the bartender over. "I've been called worse."

He had acne scars, the kind so deep you thought they might still hurt. I wanted to touch them, and he said I could. His cheek was smoother than I had thought. Like a craggy bar of soap. After last call we stumbled through the snow to his car and I let him eat me in the backseat.

On Thursdays we had Sports Hour at King's Manor. Whether they wanted to play or not, patients were gathered into the cafeteria for a game of chair volleyball.

I was pushing two chairs at once—Harold on the left, Laney on the right. They were nothing but bones in hospital gowns but it took all the strength in me to wheel them straight. My hangover felt ugly and beautiful, the pain keeping me alive.

Benny ran up to me in the hallway. "You need a hand?" he asked, and grabbed one of the handgrips.

"I can manage," I mumbled, and sped up, not wanting to talk to anyone.

"Yeah, but I'm right here." He took Laney's chair and immediately she started humming a song, her index finger conducting an imaginary orchestra. Benny and I walked side by side, his steps matching mine, even though he was tall and lanky. When we turned a corner, he said, "I've seen you before, you know."

As soon as he said this I remembered from where.

"Thursday nights? The church basement meetings?" He grinned. "Don't think I can't see you sitting in the back, shoving cookies into your pockets."

I stopped.

Benny stopped his chair, too. "What'd I do?"

I wanted to tell him that my favorite part about Narcotics Anonymous was that I could actually be anonymous. Nobody needed to know who I was before, or who

I was now. But to make a scene about this at work seemed like I'd be exposing myself even more, so I said, "Nothing," and started pushing again, maybe a little too fast.

Benny looked straight ahead. "I'm not coming on to you, if that's what you're thinking."

"I'm not."

"Some people might say that *you're* hitting on me."

We reached the cafeteria and I pulled over. "I can take it from here."

"And who could blame you? I'm the only straight guy here who's not wearing a respirator."

I waited for him to let go of Laney's chair.

Hands up in surrender, he stepped back. "You could at least laugh at my jokes."

"I'm laughing on the inside," I said, pretending to work the brakes on the chairs.

"Wow. You just made a joke." He smiled, turned on his heels, and glided down the hall as if a Gene Kelly tune was humming in his head. When he stopped to push the elevator call button, he caught me looking at him. I ducked into the cafeteria.

"Congratulations, Miss Joon." My boss was applauding me. "You are officially the slowest assistant I've ever had in my seven years at King's Manor."

He had already shoved the dining tables against the walls, except for the back wall, which was taken up by a vending machine and a double-wide door that would open up to a courtyard if it weren't winter. Heavy chains looped around the door's handles now. One glance at the patients and anyone could see that the chains were overkill.

The cafeteria was the most decorated room in the facility but somehow the trimmings, with their bold colors and their sheer demand for cheerfulness, made the room, and the people within it, depressing. We were approaching February and the walls were now taped up with giant-sized hearts, little nudes carrying bows and arrows, and gold and red letters that linked up to read, HAPPY VALENTINES DAY HAPPY VALENTINES DAY.

The patients were clustered in the center of the room

"Now, I want them divided evenly this time," my boss ordered. "Three rows of four on one side of the room, facing the three rows on the other. And can you do something about—" He stopped mid-sentence and gestured for me to wipe off Harold's chin. Harold sat in the center of the cluster, still dozing in his wheelchair. His head slumped to one side, in the same direction as his spittle, and I used the end of my shirt to clean it off. *Sleep is the sister of death*, Knowledge had said to me once, but Harold looked happy sleeping, much happier than the others, who sat with their hands dead on their laps, their milky eyes staring off into some past or at the dust particles running circles around them. They were all deflated balloons, waiting for someone—a parent, a child, anyone—to claim them again.

After I finished making the rows, my boss stood poised in the center of the aisle, clutching a whistle in one hand, a beach ball in the other. Without any warning, he blew the whistle and tossed the ball high in the air, fully expecting the patients to jump and fight for possession. The ball made a *ting* by Harold's feet. My boss clapped his hands. "C'mon, Harry, let's look alive!"

After Sports Hour I sat behind the nurses' counter, cleaning, buffing, spit-shining everything on the desk: color-coded file folders, a coffee mug filled with pens, a box of Kleenex, a PA system with a microphone. There were photos of children, mostly Filipino, trapped between the desk and its glass top. I shined that, too.

"Did you hear about Myrna in 103?"

I hadn't heard Enrique walking up. He was a vocational nurse who loved to talk about phosphate enemas. He spoke of them in surgical detail and went so far as to describe all the different sounds the patients and their bodies made. I usually avoided him, especially during meal breaks.

"Well, did you?" he asked, sitting and crossing his legs on a stool beside me.

I knew Myrna had died but didn't want to encourage him.

"She was so blocked up. It was awful." Catching his reflection on the lobby door, Enrique mussed up his hair only to smooth it back down. "I even called all three daughters. Not one of those bitches called me back." He splayed his fingers against his chest. "What a way to go. Alone and constipated. Which reminds me." Enrique spun around on the stool. "Guess what I saw today. Go ahead, guess."

"No." I yanked out a tissue, spit into it, and started polishing the PA system.

"You and the new boy, strolling down the hall together, all romantic."

"We were pushing chairs."

"Well, I thought it was sweet."

"That's because you're single."

"Speak of the devil..."

Benny came up to the counter and I almost knocked over the microphone. He and Enrique exchanged hellos and I focused on rearranging the folders on the desk, nudging the piles so the edges lined up.

"I apologize for her rude silence," Enrique said, getting up to leave. "She was raised by a pack of mimes."

I peered over the counter. Crouching behind Benny, Enrique acted out a lively conversation using his hands as puppets—his way of urging me to talk. When Benny turned around, Enrique took off, saying bye again.

Even with the counter between us, I could smell on Benny something familiar, a mixture of sweat and shoe polish. I spritzed Windex on the desk, feeling okay with the silence.

"Can I borrow a pen?"

I plucked one out from the coffee mug and handed it to him.

"Thanks." He started drumming the counter with the pen and a finger. "Hey, I saw your schedule for tonight."

I buffed the head of the microphone as if it contained

every germ in the world and pulled out hair strands that were coiled around the toggle switch. After that, I stooped under the desk to wipe down the file cabinet.

"Me, too," Benny said.

I looked up. "What?"

He folded his arms and then unfolded them. "You're getting off tonight at six, and I'm saying, me too. And since we live so close to each other we could—"

I stood up. "How do you know where I live?"

"I told you. I live across the street. I saw you going into your place once." He lodged the pen back into the mug. "Great. Now you think I'm stalking you."

"You're at my meetings and you live across the street from me and that's a coincidence?"

Some months later I would find out that nothing was a coincidence—that Benny and I were supposed to be together the way leaves are supposed to fall. A nurse walked by with two stethoscopes choked around her neck. I had said too much. Turning my back to Benny, I began organizing the shelves overflowing with tapes of classical music, magazines, and patient-birthday reminder cards for forgetful families.

"Hey, Joon," Ray said, wheeling by. "You're still coming with me tomorrow, right?"

I half nodded. I watched him roll down the long hallway. At night, under the fluorescents, the floors shined like ice, making me want to take off my shoes and skate the entire place on my socks.

"I'm still standing here," Benny said. He had brown liquid eyes. "So you want to go to the meeting or what?"

"I can't," I said, right away. "My family's in town."

"That's cool. Who's all here?"

I flipped through the cassettes and made up two quirky parents, successful cousins, and an uncle who treated us to lobster dinners and Broadway shows. "Dad gets up to sing songs about the Korean War, and Mom always has one glass too many and kisses him in front of everybody. I don't get to see them much," I added. Lying to Benny was easy because I knew he didn't believe a word of my story. It was still a good lie, though.

"Right." Benny nodded, his lips tight and disappointed. Rubbing the back of his neck, he said, "You know, we're supposed to help each other out."

That night I went home and swallowed a small vial of pills I'd lifted from the home, plus four Cokes and about thirty Pop Rocks, which took a while to tear open, the

packets being so waxy and glazed. I got into my sleeping bag and waited, for what I didn't know—my stomach
to explode, maybe. Outside a car radio faded by as some
woman shouted drunken words into the air. Benny would
be across the street, getting ready for the meeting.

Twenty minutes passed and I felt nothing, except a
tickling in my throat and chest. I tried smothering myself
with a pillow, kicked my feet like I was being murdered
and tried to slip into unconsciousness from the lack of
oxygen, but I wasn't even sleepy. Finally, I went to my pay
phone and called the operator. I told the nasal voice that
we had an emergency, that a friend of mine had swallowed a vial of—I held it up and spelled the name out
for her—and asked if it was fatal. I didn't mention the
Pop Rocks. After a few beeps a different voice came on, a
man's voice, and he explained that we were dealing with
antibiotics, for urinary tract infections. I thanked him,
hung up, and then called my dad.

The phone rang five times before he picked up.

"Hello?" he answered, again in Korean. Some song
was moaning in the background.

I slid a packet of Pop Rocks into my mouth and held
the receiver close to the sizzle on my tongue. I started
chewing.

"Who is this?" he asked. He said something else, too, but I couldn't hear with all the crackling in my mouth. I swallowed.

There was some rustling on his end—voices warped in and out, his and a woman's, maybe—before the music stopped suddenly. I pictured his short froggy legs having walked up to a stereo so he could press stop on the tape deck. When my father came back, he spoke low and determined: "I know who you are, and...let me just say how sorry I am. You don't need excuses. Nobody does. I'll have it by next week, and that's all there is to it. I know I've said this before, but this time I promise. On my life."

He went on like that and I left his words alone. I wondered what type of a loan shark he was mistaking me for. A large one, I hoped. Someone who could beat him up easily, break a bone or two. *Take a moral inventory of your soul*, my sponsor chimed in. Leaning against the wall, I focused on the sound of my father's breathing and thought about how the only word he'd said in English was "excuses," as if to blame his weakness on America. The Pop Rocks were now bombing my stomach and a string of antibiotics shot up my throat. I listened to my father apologize one more time before I hung up.

. . .

Friday night was rib night for Ray. From the nurses' station I walked past doorways flickering sheets of television light, and headed toward the smoke room, where Ray was pulling out a cigarette. Surrounded by walls made of green-tinted glass, the smoke room looked more like a dried-up aquarium, embedded with ashtray stands, oxygen tanks, and old people made of cloth. Tomorrow they were cutting off his leg.

I tapped on the glass and mouthed, "You ready?"

Since chewing ribs was out of the question for him, I shredded the meat into a blender, with extra barbecue sauce, so he could drink his meal through a straw.

Ray slurped in bed, on top of the covers. I could see on the arch of his foot the blister, now the size of a pocket watch, a crater filled with a velvety gel. I wanted to grab a spoon and scoop it out. I almost asked if it hurt but even that sounded like a promise, and who was I to be making promises?

"You're gonna have to drink up. I think they're picking you up soon," I said, walking over to the room's only window. It was starting to snow.

Ray drank silently. He held the glass with both hands and stared at the footboard as if the bed itself had done him wrong. He wouldn't look at me, and I took that to mean that he knew I wasn't going with him.

"I'll be right back," I said, and headed for the door.

"My pillow needs adjusting." He watched the TV screen even though it was off. Ray was nearly seventy but his hard blue eyes belonged to a jilted child. I returned to his bed, clicked down the rail and leaned him forward, not so gently, puffed up the pillows and set him back down.

"There," I said, and started for the door again.

"And I want to take this." With the straw still in his mouth he pointed to a book on his nightstand, a photo book about battleships. I packed it into a plastic bag he used to carry his overnight clothes.

"Okay, I'll be back," I said, rushing out. I stood out in the hallway and let the door close behind me.

"No you won't," I heard him say.

I ran home, drowning in snow. I passed random signs: Sunoco, the A&P, Yangtze River Buffet—but I couldn't

see the message in any of them. I had created a new
life for myself but didn't know what to do with it. Like
staring at a finished jigsaw puzzle, where the only thing
left to do was to mess it up again. Why couldn't Ray see
that? Why didn't he understand that the more he asked
of me, the more I realized how useless I was, how little I
belonged in the normal world? I thought about my father,
how maybe he'd felt the same. He didn't belong to this
country, to his wife, to his daughter who spoke sentences
that sounded like slimy marbles. I couldn't have sympathy for him, though. Or I didn't want to. He was my
father. I might've left my mother, but he was my father
and he'd left us first.

The snow kept coming, erasing the city, trying to
make all things equal and white, except on the boulevard,
where cars drew themselves a railway of slush. It was
cold. The wind was freezing my face into a mask. A bus
roared by, giving me a blur of greenish windows and an
ad for Irish Spring below them. When my father had first
seen the commercial—a man carving a bar of soap with
a jackknife—he thought it was an ad for the knife and
didn't see what the big deal was, a knife cutting up a bar
of soap. *Knives from Korea can cut any soap*, he said. My

mother laughed, and I did, too, but wives and daughters weren't supposed to laugh at fathers. He dragged me by the hair to a playground near our home and ordered me to hang from the chin-up bar. We had changed countries but he didn't want to change. He slid his belt out from his pants and whipped me in front of all the kids in the park. Most were my age. They watched from their seesaws and swings but I couldn't look at them, at least not in the eyes. I studied the barrel buttons on their coats, their galoshes paused on a hopscotch square. I looked beyond the playground's chain-link fence, out onto Eastchester Road, where small heads inside buses and cars streamed past, all of them in profile, looking straight ahead and not seeing a goddamn thing.

That night, with my father on the phone, I stood holding a kitchen knife over my wrist. With the sound of him apologizing into my ear, begging for one more day, I took a deep breath and thought, *Free the veins*.

"Hello? Are you still there?" my father asked, and I sliced.

The knife clanged as it hit the concrete floor, and the phone swung from my shoulder. I looked at the damage. It was nothing more than a paper cut, the thin line of blood pearling on my wrist looking more like jewelry than death closing in. Still, I was sweating, could feel my heart fighting, and I wanted to scream but couldn't with my father still on the phone. I picked him up again. "Please, I'm begging you," he said, or something like that, and this time I steadied my wrist against the phone and leaned forward on one leg so I could use the force of my weight to slice down harder. My hands were shaking. I lined up the blade into the line of the cut. "I'll give you everything I have," he cried as I took in a breath and closed my eyes. I had no head, no legs, not even a body. All that existed was the sting on my wrist and a floating image of Ray lying in a hospital bed with some doctor standing over him, preparing to saw off his leg. I exhaled for as long as I could and waited for courage to strike.

When I heard the knocking I thought it was coming from my father's end. I opened my eyes and saw my reflection on the phone. With my bangs covered in sweat, I didn't recognize myself.

"Who is it?" I whispered. Nobody answered, which made me realize I was nowhere near the door.

"Hello?" my father said in my ear. "Who is this?" he asked, in English this time, and he didn't sound scared anymore. He was back to his old self, acting as if the world owed him something.

"I gotta go, Dad," I said, hanging up.

I didn't care who was at the door, what they had or what they were going to do to me when I let them in. The fact that it was Benny didn't surprise me any. He didn't ask questions—he just stood there, not minding the cold and letting me hug and kiss him as if I owned him, as if I had every right in the world to dig into his body and hide forever. I let him in, and into my sleeping bag, and just before we were about to make love, he rolled out his gear.

The syringe. The lighter. The shoe polish. The bottom of a soda can. As the fleck of shoe polish disappeared into our chunks, and our chunks, the size of two Tic Tacs, disappeared into our water, my father's struggles here became clear to me. The country was new and strange. It unanchored him. But the liquor was the same, and his habits were the same. He merely drifted toward things familiar—drinking, cheating—paths that never questioned who he was and why he was there. And who was I to judge. The sweat on my arm turned as cold as seashells, and I waited for Benny to set up my hit but told him I'd shoot it myself since we didn't know each other that well.

And when the rush speared my veins, freeing every

muscle, I gasped what must've been a skyful of air and let the warm piss flow out of me. I let it soak my underwear, my sleeping bag, and maybe Benny, who was now lying by my side in his own world of faith. The hit took me wherever I wanted. *I ever tell you about the Parachute Jump?* Ray had asked once. We were at the bench, smoking. *It's in Coney Island. They called it Brooklyn's Eiffel Tower. You sit on this thing and they pull you up by cable, so high I swear you're making deals with God.* He turned his head toward me. He thought I'd said something but I hadn't. *That's where I met Helen, my wife. She and I got paired to go up that thing. She wasn't the prettiest, but that hair...it was so red against that big blue sky, and all the way up she giggled and smiled at me, like we'd already done things our parents would've killed us for. Then BAM! The next thing you know, I saw my future in those eyes of hers. I just did. I heard our kids laughing her laugh. The Thanksgiving dinners, the trips to the Grand Canyon.* He took a drag of his cigarette and let out a long trail. *Now, where the fuck is she when I need her?* He dumped out the plastic bag and let the crumbs snow on the birds. *Where the fuck is she?*

"I'm here," I told the ceiling.

"What?" Benny asked, before falling into a fit of

laughter that echoed as I seesawed up to the invisible sun, above the birds of Coney Island where the Parachute Jump pulled me to the top until the noise of the board-walk below faded and all I could hear was the sound of my heart and the wind rattling the cables. I looked over an ocean that was as blue as the sky and said, I'm right here.

In the Tombs

This was what I remembered.

That once I found my mother lying completely still in our vegetable garden, between rows of napa cabbage and pickling cucumbers. She hadn't changed out of her nurse's uniform —white shoes, white stockings, a long-sleeved white dress that stopped just above her knees. The left side of her nursing cap was bobby-pinned to her hair but the right side had come undone, as if that spot on her skull had erupted and blown the cap off onto the dirt. The sun had reddened her eyelids, her forearms, the hands that clasped her Bible to her chest. I was maybe seven years old, and I wasn't worried. I'd seen her like this before. Every time my father left us. And every time she kicked him out. Once, I'd found her in our bathtub, with no water, fully dressed, pearl earrings, makeup, and dinner party shoes, again with the Bible. Another time, under our dinette set, her arms as stiff as sticks by her side, the Bible butterflied open on her face, as if she were trying to breathe in the words. Both times I sat beside her and played jacks or made origami flowers or quizzed myself with flashcards, until she woke up.

But this was the first time she had pretended to be dead *outside* our home. An ant crawled up the tracks of her white zipper, which ran along the center of her chest and opened to a V at the base of her neck, following the lines of her collarbone. I tickled her chin and laughed at the possibility of her laughing, but when she didn't, I thought nothing of it. I plopped down and played in the dirt, made mounds of mud, dug up tiny pebbles and lined them up like pearls around her neck. I placed my hand on her tummy and piled the mud high on top of that hand before pulling my hand out slowly, leaving behind a tall brown igloo. Using the stem of a cucumber plant, I poked a hole at the opposite end, turning the igloo into a tunnel, through which the tracks of her zipper traveled. I piled dirt onto her legs to make mountain ridges and clumped mud on both of her shoes to build twin volcanoes. Families made of sticks and stems lived along her body, which was surrounded by towers of cucumber until the flash flood came (with the help of a watering can) and drowned my little village.

The sky turned twilight and all the townspeople were dead. And my mother lay still through it all. It was getting dark. A part of me thought to wake her up but that was the most time I'd spent with her in a while. A few lines of mud streaked her face. Still, she looked beautiful. My father had once said she was too beautiful but he had said it like it was a curse. Somebody in the neighborhood started cooking fish, and the smell made me think it was time to go inside.

I nudged her shoulder. She didn't wake up. A light came on across our driveway, and a second later Mrs. McCommon, our next-door neighbor, appeared in her kitchen window. She stood over the sink, rinsing something, and her eyes took snapshots of us as she talked on the phone, her head tilted to one side to keep the receiver from slipping. She laughed, and her lips stretched like a rubber band being pulled. It seemed fair to hate her. I looked up. No stars and no clouds, the sky was a sheet of cellophane, showing off a shade of blue that made everything

below it—our garden, our driveway, my mother's skin—
seem bruised and untouchable. I couldn't see the moon. I
went inside.

Without washing my hands, I ate shrimp-flavored
chips while hopping on the couch, from cushion to cushion. When I got bored with that, I put on *Swan Lake*,
raised the volume to ten, and twirled through the house
until I was sticky with sweat and the needle on the
turntable skated the center, filling my head with static.
I climbed our carpeted stairs and slid down on my ass
to the beat of that static, and when I got tired of that,
I hugged my bag of chips and watched TV. *Happy Days*
was on but I couldn't concentrate. She'd never pretended
this long.

I snuck into the kitchen, kept the light off, climbed
up onto the counter, and peeked out the window with my
forehead touching the cold glass. There she was. In her
white uniform she looked like a patch of snow melting
in the dirt. Except for the light from Mrs. McCommon's
front porch, the garden was dark. I fogged up the windowpane and drew a rectangle around her body. My
mother was the size of my pencil case. I wondered what
would happen if she had to pee. She would have to move
for that. A car coughed and crawled onto our driveway,

backed out, and climbed up the ramp for the Bruckner Expressway, where a siren sped past us, leaving a long echo.

Maybe that was what had woken her up. My mother's legs broke through the dirt as she bent her knees and stood, blocking the porch light enough to draw a long shadow of herself on the dirt. With the light directly behind her, her hair and face disappeared, and for a long second she looked headless. She didn't brush off her uniform. She didn't shake off her hair. She didn't clap her hands clean. She just came up the back stairs and through the back kitchen door as if she were following a smell.

"I know what you did to me," she said, passing by.

I know what you did to me.

This was what I thought about when my public defender told me that my mother was dead. We were in the interview room at the Manhattan Detention Complex, also known as the Tombs, and he said it so matter-of-factly that I wondered how big this news was and how big my reaction should or shouldn't be. I couldn't think. I was coming down from something and my brain felt like an old, chewed-up piece of gum. We were in a room the size of a car, with barely enough space for a table, two chairs, and a tall sign framed in plastic. The sign began with DETAINEE SHALL NOT ACCEPT . . . followed by a long list of prohibited items.

"Are you sure?" I asked.

"Am I sure what?"

"That she's dead. Sometimes she fakes it."

He looked through my folder. "She's been dead for six months."

"I guess that would be hard to pull off." I said this and smiled a little to let him think I was joking. "I mean, that's impossible, right?"

"You lost me."

"To fake a death. That would be crazy, right?"

"I think so."

"Yeah," I said, but couldn't shut up. "Are you sure she wasn't breathing? You checked her pulse and everything?"

"Well, I wasn't there, Joon."

"Of course you weren't. Nobody's saying you were." I sat up to show I was ready to move on, and by the way he shut my folder and folded his hands on top of it, I could tell he was ready, too. His name was Louis Burby, and he looked exactly like his name. Sweaty nose, veiny skin, small, newborn eyes. His head was shaped like an egg and it sat on top of his torso, which was basically a larger egg. I liked him because he always got me out, and because we swapped favors. He bought me smokes or Donettes or sometimes clothes from The Salvation Army. And I gave him my feet.

He scooted his chair back as far as it would go. "Can I see them?" he asked, peering under the table. "I did look up your mom for you."

"I didn't ask you to."

He took off his glasses and cleaned them with his tie. "I can probably get the judge to give you credit for time served."

CTS sounded good. It meant I could leave after sentencing. I looked past him and at the small, wire-caged window on the door. "In the parking lot, after my release," I said. "And I want a Big Mac. With fries this time."

"Of course," he said, grabbing his briefcase. "I can't wait to see them."

This was what the holding tank was like.

A television bolted high up in the corner said: *I didn't know you were alive!*

"Aw, yes you did, you a liar!" a woman shouted up at

the screen, her voice husky from smoke and drink. "She's all acting like she never heard of amnesia."

I remember everything, the television said.

"Shit. You're in for it now, and she ain't gonna forget to kick your ass this time," the woman said. She was one of the lucky ones. She had a spot on the bench. I stood in the back corner, next to a girl who was talking on the pay phone, her free hand clutching the short metal cord. The cell was crowded. I counted the heads around me, length times width. There were sixty of us. Some on the floor, some on the bench, and some shared a mattress by the front, under the blaring TV. Heads bobbed to stay awake or to stay asleep. Most of the women worked the streets and the cell smelled like coconut tanning lotion. I thought about my mother. What she would think if she could see me here, if she could smell on me the failures of sixty women. She was dead now. Her nose was filled with dirt. I felt something in my chest for her but I kept the feeling small. Jail wasn't the place to have a breakdown. I needed a cave. I needed a long subway ride.

The girl next to me was now hollering into the pay phone. She had orange hair with only half of it cornrowed. The other half shot up from her head as she screamed at the pay phone's rotary dial like it was the face of her enemy.

"You better shake a leg, Leo, 'cause check this out—I don't appreciate your little white-piece-of-trash-ass *bitch* telling my son that she's his stepmommy. You tell that white dirty *bitch* that she ain't shit to my motherfucking son, and the bitch better stay in her motherfucking place before I catch that bitch and beat the fuck outta her. You get me?"

"Somebody shut her up!" the husky voice said. She stretched her neck toward the television set.

". . . and you better check that bitch and tell her she ain't shit to my motherfucking son, and if I ever hear *my son* saying a word about *that bitch*, I'm gonna get you *and* that bitch, you dumb ass nigga." The girl slammed the phone down. Then she slammed it down again and again, and maybe six more times after that.

I was in jail for shoplifting baby food, those tiny jars of Gerber carrots, Gerber peas, and two tubs of Enfamil I'd lumped under a blanket in my stroller. The owner of the fruit and vegetable store, a Korean man in a pink polo shirt, grabbed my arm in the middle of the sidewalk. He jerked me around, pushed me along with one hand, the stroller with the other, back into the store and down the fruit aisle, where shoppers watched me with tight eyes.

By the pyramid of oranges I turned on the drama. I cried that I was trying to be a good mother, trying to feed my little baby girl, and you can't blame me for wanting to feed my baby. It felt good to be a tragic hero. I was not one for making scenes but I played for the crowd, all of five ladies, because it was my only chance at being let go. The owner yanked me hard and put his face close enough to remind me of my father's anger. He asked what the baby's name was and I guess I stuttered a second too long. "That's what I thought," he said, and then in Hanguk he asked: "Are you Korean?"

I looked into his eyes, those angry black bugs, and pretended he was talking gibberish. "What? Speak English, man!" I shouted, and turned to my audience. "You're in America now."

And for that I deserved time. I knew it even then.

I stole the baby food for Benny. He repackaged the jars into boxes and sold them back to the grocery store owners.

While standing in the back of the cell, waiting for arraignment, I pictured my mother in that grocery store. I imagined my really having a baby and having to steal food, not only for my child but for all abandoned children in the state of New York. And then I imagined my mother hugging me, being proud of me for having sacrificed myself for the good of the children. In another version, my mother and I both stole—we were both tragic heroes.

A guard walked up to the cell and called my name. "It's showtime!" he shouted, without looking up from his clipboard. I made my way to the front, put my hands on the bars so he could cuff me while I was still inside. His fingers were cold.

"Sayonara," somebody said as I stepped out.

With his hand choking the back of my arm, he guided me down a long hallway, not saying much, not doing much, until we came upon a door. He let go of me to open the door with a key and then gripped me again as we went down another hallway. Trophies encased in glass. Slick photos of police chiefs. Plaques with names engraved on small, golden plates. He nodded or gave clipboard-salutes to people who passed us, and the key ring looped to his belt jangled against his hips. The rhythm bugged me. It was too constant. Too military. The inside of his ear was too polished, and his face was too rigid. I thought I could see nuts and bolts on the corners of his jawline. I hadn't thought to be bothered by his looks, but now, while walking down what felt like a maze of offices, I felt weak next to him. We turned another corner, and then another, that led us along beige-colored walls lined with photos of Rikers Island.

"You're taking me to the judge, right?"

"Something like that," he said, and kept his focus ahead of him.

We reached the end of the hall and walked into a stairwell that smelled like rust. His keys echoed. It was dark in there. The soles of his shoes squealed on the metal steps as we walked down two flights. It felt like we were underground.

I asked him where we were headed.

He laughed a little. "*We* aren't headed anywhere," he said, tightening his grip on my arm.

I didn't like his voice. It had the flat tone of someone wanting to teach me a lesson. At the bottom of the stairs we walked through a steely door, which spit us out into the loudest sound I'd ever heard. The noise was like the workings of a thousand heating vents. Cardboard boxes, some stacked three high, clogged our path. Black pipes ran along the ceiling, spewing out steam, leaking on us as we walked past upturned chairs and drawerless desks cluttered with telephones and extension cords.

My sneakers slipped on a soggy file folder stuck to the floor. "Where is this?" I shouted. The cop didn't hear or he ignored me. He wouldn't even look my way. The light switches had been gutted out, office doors lay sideways on the ground, and the walls looked to be dripping oil. No framed pictures, no trophies, no police chiefs. We were alone. "Where are we?" I asked again but knew it was useless. He would kill me and no one would hear me die. No one would find me. I wanted to scream but instead I jerked free from his grip and took a step back. I didn't bother running. "Please," I said, but I couldn't hear my own voice. He grabbed ahold of my cuffs and yanked me toward him, shouting, "Where do you think you're going?" He opened a door and tossed me into an office.

The light was too bright. It felt as though we had stepped inside a bulb. I squinted and shaded my eyes with my wrists, as a group of girls, handcuffed together and sitting in a circle, slowly came into focus.

"Welcome! You must be Joon-Mee?" a woman said, getting up from her chair. I looked at the guard. "Go on," he said, and nudged me toward the woman. She had on jeans, a tight cable-knit sweater, and a name tag that read: *Hello. My name is Trish.* She offered me her hand for a handshake. I raised my cuffs.

"Oh, right. Sorry. I'm new at this," she said, and motioned for me to take a seat. The guard plugged me into the circle, cuffing me to girls on my left and right, and told the counselor woman that he'd be right out in the hall. It took me a while to readjust my thinking of him, to stop seeing him as a rapist killer.

"Maybe you'd like to say something about yourself?" the counselor asked.

I shook my head.

It ended up being one of those outreach programs, where they selected girls who looked as if they might have a chance at changing the course of their lives. Some of them talked. I knew better.

"He's my man and I'm gonna stand by him no matter what," a girl said.

The counselor tilted her head. "Even if that lands you in prison?"

"Prison don't scare me."

"Just so we're clear..." The counselor pointed to the floor. Her nails were painted pink. "This isn't prison. This is jail and it is nothing compared to prison."

"What the fuck you know?" another girl said.

The guard tapped the door. "Don't make me come in there."

The session went on. One girl cried. Other girls listened by rolling their eyes. I listened, too. They sounded stupid to me, and the more they talked, the more I turned the volume down and zoomed in on the details of our circle—the dried scabs on the knees of a girl across from me, her dirty shoes, our dirty shoes, the stained hems of our jeans, our greasy hair. I tried to look for the best-dressed girl in the room but it was like trying to find dirt in mud. I couldn't tell me from them. Not in this room.

"My mom writes letters all the time now," another girl said, "but that's 'cause she's locked up and she's clean. Soon as she's out, I never hear from her. That's how she is. I hope they never let her out."

Hearing this, I decided that my mother being dead was a good thing. Good for her. Now she would never know about this, about how I had turned out. Eighteen and in jail. I had run away for my sake, but maybe a part of me had stayed away for hers. I did talk to her once, at a coffee shop. Benny had said we needed money. He wanted us to go to California and start fresh there. In Los Angeles. So I called her up and she agreed to meet me. Her voice sounded too rational, and calm, as if confirming an appointment with her dentist. I hadn't seen her in a while, since the night behind the bushes at her hospital. I recognized her right away, though. When she entered the coffee shop, she pulled out a tissue from her purse, placed three dabs across her forehead, two dabs against each nostril, a dab each for the corners of her lips. I watched from a table in the back. Even from that distance I could tell how much she had changed. She was too thin. Her collarbone looked more like a hanger for the dress she had on, the hem of which barely flowed as she walked toward me, taking tiny, composed steps like she used to down the church aisle, looking for space along the pews. All life had been scooped out of her once-full cheeks, and her hands, which had trouble pulling out the chair across from me, were nothing more than bundles of kindling.

"Hi, Mom."

She sat down. No makeup, no jewelry. Her eyes were dark tunnels. Once in a while they shifted within the frames of her thinning lashes, a glance at the waitress taking an order, a look at the cigarette vending machine, a blank stare at the two women holding hands across the aisle.

"Mom," I said, louder this time.

She turned to me, perhaps noticing me for the first time. Her eyes welled up.

"Your father's missing," she said, strangling the tissue in her hand.

I asked her what she was talking about.

"He's gone." She looked lost. Or like she had lost something she shouldn't have. "He's missing," she said again.

I wanted to shove a napkin in her mouth to stop her from saying it. Without raising my voice I informed her that he had left us years ago.

"Do you know where he is?" she asked.

I shook my head.

"In Staten Island. Living with some woman from our church."

"He's not missing if you know where he is." As soon as I said this, I realized that it wasn't true. My mother had been missing for a very long time, even when we lived together, and she was missing now, even sitting just across from me.

"I want you to go see him. Today." She pinched her nose with the tissue. "I want you to bring him back. You're good at that."

"I haven't done that in a long time."

"You have to do this for me," she whispered. "You have to."

The look in her eyes, so wanting and frightened and

tired, like someone on a hunger strike, holding out for something that'll never happen.

"I love him," she said.

I replaced *him* with *you.*

"I want him to come back," she said.

"I know," I said.

"He loves my cooking."

She never cooked when he wasn't around. A few times I had found her late at night, standing by the kitchen counter in her pajamas, chopping things—carrots, onions, meat—only to slide them off the cutting board and into the trash can.

"So you'll do this for me?" she asked. "You'll go see him?"

I wondered if she had ever thought of me as missing, or if she saw how thin I looked, the knots in my hair, my scraped-up hands. Or Benny sitting at the counter, slurping soup, bouncing his knees, watching all of this with only his agenda in mind. *Los Angeles. Sunny Angeles.*

In the end, I told her that I'd go see him, my father. I lied for the money.

She dumped her purse upside down and opened up, not her wallet, but her compact. As she powdered her nose with hummingbird hands I realized she was preparing for my father, as if I might pull him out from my pocket any minute. "I can't have him see me like this," she said, and smeared on a dark shade of rouge. The longer she saw herself in the mirror, the more she seemed on the verge of tears. "I look terrible, don't I?"

Her lips were now bruised and crooked. "You look beautiful," I said, to a small brown stain trapped in the plastic of the table. My throat carried the weight of all the times I had been asked to tell her this.

"Your father used to say that," she said, and smiled a distant smile.

I nodded in agreement and then asked for money.

"Oh," she said, snapping back to the moment, and opened her wallet. I could see Benny behind my mother, standing up to try to see how much I would get. She handed me a five. Benny snuck up close enough to see the bill, at which point he shoved both thumbs toward the ceiling to show he wanted more. But my mother said that was all she had. I believed her.

When I said goodbye I knew I wouldn't see her again. Maybe she knew it, too. When she got up, she took a step toward me and for a second it seemed as though we might hug. My shoulders stiffened. We never hugged. That was something we didn't do. She looked right at me—me in my jeans and T-shirt I'd been wearing for maybe a week—and after a good look, she simply gave me her hand. It felt like a warm dying bird.

While daisy-chained to the circle of girls at the detention complex, I pictured my mother again, lying completely still in that garden. *I know what you did to me*, she had said back then. I still didn't know what that meant. But this I understood: although she had me and all those vegetables around her, she only wanted my father's love.

"That's all the money she had," I said to Benny that day, but soon realized that I had actually said these very words out loud to the circle of handcuffed girls, who were all now staring at me.

"I'm sorry, Joon? Did you say something?" the counselor asked.

"That's all she had," I said, the words feeling pebbly in my throat.

"That's all who had?"

That was all she had and she did her best. That was the truth. That was what the counselor would've said if I had opened up. Here was another truth: my mother was all I had. And now she was dead and I was alone to wonder if I had done my best.

. . .

When the session was over, the guard took my arm again, gentler this time, and walked me back to the holding tank.

"So, what'd you think?" he asked.

I didn't feel like talking. "You really scared me back there," I said, giving him a sideways glance, noticing for the first time a small medallion, the size of a quarter, next to his badge. I couldn't read much of it except the years 1950–1953.

"What you should be scared about is what you heard in the circle."

"It didn't sound all that bad."

He shook his head, as if I'd disappointed him.

"Why are you looking at me like that?" I asked.

He yanked me aside. "I'm just curious. You notice anything strange about your holding tank?"

I told him I didn't know what he was talking about, and that the only thing I saw was a woman talking to a television and a girl chewing her man out on the pay phone.

"Think again," he said, and pushed down on my cuffs so I couldn't lift my hands.

I told him he was hurting me.

"Listen," he whispered, and scanned the hallway. "A lot of those women, in your cell, they're supposed to be there. They grew up in shit holes worse than anything we got here. I understand that. I get it. They don't know any better. But you..." His voice trailed off. "Where are you from?"

"The Bronx," I said.

"No. I'm asking you, what are you?"

I knew where this was going but I told him anyway. "I'm Korean."

"Korea. That's what I thought," he said. "Do you know what percentage of prisoners are Korean?"

"A hundred percent," I said. "In Korea."

"Forget it." He pushed me to start walking. "I'd like to see you be so funny when they drop you at Rikers."

"I know what you're doing," I told him.

"Bet you think you know a lot of things."

"You're trying to scare me straight. But don't worry. I can take care of myself."

"I don't give a shit what you do," he said. "Your PD's the one who recommended you for counseling, not me."

"Well, I didn't want counseling, so..."

We walked down yet another endless hallway, the

silence between us like a third wall. I had disappointed him—someone was disappointed in me—and for reasons I didn't fully understand back then, this made me happy in a quiet sort of way. When we got back to the cell, I told him I was sorry. He refused to notice me. He uncuffed me, put me in without a word, and called out another name from his clipboard. A few seconds later, he and the girl were gone.

The holding tank now smelled like old mayonnaise. It felt as though I'd been gone for days until I heard the girl with orange hair still hollering about her son. Instead of screaming into the pay phone, she now stood in the center of the cell and preached to the women, even though most of them were asleep and leaning on one another like fallen dominoes.

"Why do people have to mess with my son?" she asked us. I settled into a spot on the floor, by the back again. "I mean, that's *my* son. I gave birth to him. He came out of *my* vagina. That makes him mine. That's what that means. You got something coming out of your vagina, that's all yours."

"She's got a point," somebody said.

"Amen," somebody else said.

. . .

Whenever I got released from jail I wanted to do things I'd never done before. Like go see a wrestling match or hitchhike across the country or lie down in a stream at the Bronx Botanical Gardens and make the water bend around me. This feeling lasted about forty-five minutes, the time it took for me to be released, reclaim my things, and walk across the street to a parking lot where I knew my public defender would be, waiting in his car.

Louis leaned over and opened the passenger door. I got in, and immediately he raised the armrest between us and lowered the radio volume. The car smelled of fries and pinecones.

"Here, dig in," he said, passing me a McDonald's bag.

I told him thanks and asked if he got me ketchup.

"It should be in the bottom." He reached into the bag himself, pulled out a packet, tore it open with his teeth, and squirted the ketchup on the fries for me.

"I got something else for you." He held out a small plastic bag and I told him he should open it since my hands were full. With a sheepish grin he pulled out four bottles of polish: Ruby Red, Pink Frost, Coral Blue, and Plum.

"You didn't have to do that," I said, but was glad that

he did. I kissed him on the cheek and asked if he was
ready.

He said he was.

I set my burger on the dashboard and took off my
sneakers.

"Don't forget the socks."

I peeled them off as slowly as I would a scab and
handed them over. He smelled them, quietly, then placed
one on his lap and one on the dashboard. I clicked my
seat back, balanced the burger and fries on my belly,
and put my feet up on the dash, right on top of the sock.
Louis sighed. Like he'd been saved from danger. He
never touched them. And he never touched himself. He
just stared at them, always on the dash, always with an
expression that was somewhere between grief and curi-
osity. Sometimes I thought he might cry, which made me
wonder if he actually enjoyed our meetings. If he liked
himself during, and after.

I finished my burger. I thanked him for the polish and
told him I had to go.

"Hold on." He reached for his briefcase in the back
and pulled out a copy of a police report. It was about my
mom, on the night of her death. Only then did I realize
that I had forgotten to ask him how she had died. I took

the report. Two pages of the accident. One page from
my father, giving his statement. I didn't know if I should
thank Louis or punch him in the face for giving me information I didn't want to own. I did neither and got out of
the car.

This was the way I saw it.

Sometime after our meeting at the coffee shop, my
mother and my father reconciled. He came back to her,
to our house. He had his suitcase with him, which he
placed on their bed before stepping into the shower. My
mother, who probably didn't know what to do with all that
energy that comes with winning someone back, opened
up his suitcase to unpack his belongings. She couldn't
have predicted her reaction. She couldn't have prepared
herself to see his undershirts and underwear crisply
folded, socks rolled into potatoes, and pants ironed and
folded in threes. In seeing these items, she recognized
that only a woman could've packed them with such care.
And the thought of another woman having touched his
underthings shot her to insanity. As soon as my father
stepped out of the shower, my mother threw him out for

what must have been the sixth time in their marriage. But as he was driving away, she changed her mind, as she sometimes did, and got into her car to go after him. She didn't even make it out of our neighborhood. Three blocks away she ran a red light and a truck crashed into her cheekbones, shoulders, and pelvis, finally breaking her into the pieces she'd always felt inside.

Years later, when I bumped into my father on the subway, none of this came up. He placed his combination briefcase between his legs and gripped the railing above him, his body turned to the man to his right. They talked seriously, in Korean, and he didn't see me for a long while. They both had on suits, and his looked thin and silky—tiny bits of glitter lived inside the fabric. I was sitting one seat to his left. Our knees were inches apart. He smelled familiar, and maybe it was this that compelled me to tug on his pants and wave up to him. He looked genuinely stunned for a second, and then asked, "How are you? You doing good?" I couldn't decide what to be upset about first. The fact that he was speaking to me in English or that he'd asked these questions as though I were a business acquaintance. I told him I was fine.

He didn't introduce me to the man beside him and

instead talked about himself, how he was in real estate, how the business was booming, how he had recently donated five thousand dollars to his church, the largest church in Queens. At the start of each sentence he would look at me, but for the majority of his speeches, he would turn and address the man. It was clear he was trying to impress this man, and that made me feel pity for my father but not the kind I could enjoy. He called himself the mayor of Koreatown and went on about how people revered him. When he ate at restaurants, everyone came by to bow and pay him respect, like the old days in Korea, he told us, his voice trumping the sounds of the subway. He wanted every commuter to hear, these complete strangers who probably didn't understand a single word of what he was saying because of his accent. I told him that I was happy for him, and that his English was improving.

When the train slowed, he and the man grabbed their belongings. My father sidestepped toward the doors and told me to call him if I needed anything. He tapped my shoulder while saying this, and I wanted to grab ahold of his hand and tell him really simple things, like how good it was to see him and how I had forgotten the smell of Old Spice. But his hand left and the doors opened and before my words could find my throat, he and his combination briefcase walked off the train without giving me his phone number. We never once mentioned my mother.

What We Had

And one day I woke up with Benny next to me and, next to him, a girl I didn't know. We were living in a motel where black wires snaked down from a hole in the ceiling, guiding the rain onto the foot of our bed. The girl could've been anybody. A teller, a waitress, a cashier from the A&P waiting for a bus in the storm. Anyone willing to drown with him. I sat up and looked for their gear. It was on the floor, soaking in a Dixie cup, the water a little pink from the blood. Q-tip heads. Rubbing alcohol. A large soupspoon with the handle wrapped in a Band-Aid. Things we used to share. The room smelled of warm vinegar. Somewhere under our blankets the radio sang low, muffled enough for me to think that the sound was coming from somewhere in my chest.

She was blond like the others and he was hugging her, wrapping his long white body around hers in a tight braid, wanting to dream her dreams. She was smiling. She had thin skin. I could see the system of veins on the back of her hand. And the black hole just above her wrist. A pencil mark. A start of a scab. His back was to me and I took that to mean something. I reached over them across the bed to grab his cigarettes and a box of matches on the nightstand. I coughed, cleared my throat twice, and rattled the tiny box like I was trying to guess what was inside it. When he didn't wake, I struck a match and dropped it in his ear.

He shot up, slapping the side of his face, over and over, like a dog. I slipped out of bed without saying a word.

"Fuck, what was that?" He rubbed his eyes and then stared blankly at the TV before rubbing his eyes some more.

"Maybe you were dreaming," I said.

Outside, the rain tried to break through the glass. I put on all the clothes I owned—two pairs of socks, three tees, a pair of pants, two sweaters, and my jacket.

"I'm not coming back," I said.

He lay back down with eyes already shut, pulled the girl in closer, draped her arm across his cracker-thin chest, and their bodies took over the bed and the pillow that had held the shape of me.

I left without slamming the door.

It was sunny and raining. Blades of white light cut through the clouds and shined on the glassy tubes of rain as they streaked the air and tapped my jean jacket. I stood across the street from the motel and counted to twenty, and then forty, to the beat of the neon sign blinking next to our window. PSYCHIC, the sign said, again and again. I counted past sixty without much thought and went up to a hundred. Twice. First in English, and then Korean. Benny didn't come out for me. I knew he wouldn't but I still wanted to make sure. Two-legged umbrellas crossed the street, threading themselves between cars and dump trucks and vans that were honking at a bus making a lazy turn. My hair felt stiff and cold. Maybe I would've waited years for Benny if the weather had been different, if I hadn't looked down and noticed the rainwater rushing against the curb, and the Barbie head, her hair splayed like wings above her face, stuck behind a to-go carton lying on its side. The water slid over her eyes and nose and lips that kissed the carton, until the weight of all that came before her propelled her down Hemming Street. I started walking. It was as good a direction as any.

The traffic lights flashed red and yellow as I wandered past liquor signs, plastic cakes, trees of discount shoes, and faded hairstyle posters behind barred windows, and soon the storefronts made way for a deserted lot, a tire shop, an abandoned gas station, and a White Castle that stood like a tooth on that block of browns. Through the windowpane I saw a guy sitting alone at the counter with his shoulders slumped and his head bowed over a coffee cup as if it were raining inside and only on him. I kept on, past bus stop shelters, a porn shop, a second-story apartment window taped with pages from a coloring book, until I walked through a heavy wooden door and stepped into O'Brien's.

The darkness always surprised me. At the bar I uncrumpled my last ten dollars onto the counter and gave Henry my order, not ashamed of the morning hour. My jacket was soaked. I took it off and shook out the rain.

"Still flooding out there?" Henry asked.

I told him it was.

"I love it. Gets the scum off the streets," he said, and took a swig of beer.

Henry was always a pint ahead of everybody. That, along with the fat on him, made him move slow, but I didn't mind because he also counted slow when pouring my drink. Three fingers, no ice. O'Brien's was a cold tomb with no music or darts or Pac-Man, but the smell of sticky beer and Henry's cigar warmed the place in spirit. On the door, a small diamond-shaped window funneled the bar's only daylight onto Henry's balding head and the lineup of liquor stacked behind him. Above the bottles hung a huge sign made of scrap wood: *God has a soft spot for all who enter. When you leave you're on your own.* Two old souls who could've been twins slouched at the other end of the bar, picking up their chins long enough to raise their pints at me. As if I were one of them. I'm just sitting here, I don't live here, I thought, and smiled and returned the toast. Then I realized I wasn't living anywhere now.

The front door opened and let in a slice of light. Before I could turn to see who it was, Henry was punching the air with his cigar. "Get outta here, you crazy fuck."

A skinny old man stood by the doorway. "Have you seen my Mary?" he asked, a quiet panic trapped in his voice. He had on a shriveled suit that was gray and drippy, like his beard, like his long and clumpy hair. He looked cold and confused. I had no room for this man's confusion, and I might've ignored him except that on the crook of his elbow he carried a green grocery basket, just big enough for the wet dog shivering in it. The dog howled something long and meaningful until the old man eased him with a pat on the head. His fingers were arthritic, marbles stuck in each joint. "Have you seen my Mary?" he whispered, just to me this time.

I told him no, and that I didn't know who she was. Disappointed with my answer, the dog lay down, and it was in the way he fell, a partial collapse onto his side, that made me look away.

"You wanna see me count, is that it?" Henry flipped open a hinged slab of the counter, and that was enough of a threat. The door closed and the wedge of light disappeared. Henry plugged the cigar back into his mouth and returned to his pals, boasting about all the harm he would've inflicted on the old man. I drank and tried to picture who Mary could be. Maybe she was just another dog. I hoped it wasn't. Dogs look so scared when they're lost, or worse, when they're hungry.

.   .   .

Don't feed him, Benny had said to me when I wanted to share our lunch with a stray. This was a few months back. A black mutt had followed a trail that led him to us sitting on the sidewalk, in front of the motel, devouring a small bucket of Kentucky Fried Chicken I'd bought for us. We hadn't eaten in I don't know how long.

"I can see every rib," I said, touching the dog's side. His coat reminded me of dry grass.

"All you'd be doing is giving him false hope." Benny grabbed the dog's snout. "When it's over, it's over, and you know that, don't ya, pal?"

The mutt didn't fight Benny's grip. Instead he stuck his tongue out sideways and licked Benny's hand, the look in his eyes flickering from joy to uncertainty, not knowing whether to be grateful for the touch or to run for his life.

"I'm going to feed him," I said.

Benny shook his head but put his hand out, as if to introduce the dog to me. "Go ahead. You're free to do whatever you want."

On the ground I put out the last two pieces, a leg and a thigh, and the dog quickly cracked the bones using his side teeth. It felt good to watch him eat. As if I was the one getting full. Benny went up to our room and I followed, keeping the feeling to myself for the rest of the night and falling asleep with it.

And the good feeling was still there the next morning when Benny and I woke up early to go on a mission to score. We got out of bed, slapped on some clothes, and stepped out onto the quiet street. The sky was still black and secretive, holding back its light from the buildings, the manhole covers, and all the sidewalks, including the one where the dog lay. I almost tripped over him. We were about a block from the motel. He was on his side, a little dish of blood under his mouth.

"Chicken bones. It tears up the insides," Benny said, and walked on ahead. "I told you not to feed him."

I touched his chest to see if I could feel something alive. I wanted to make sure, but really, what I wanted was time to understand.

"You coming?" Benny called, without turning around.

"You want some gum?" Henry asked one of the regulars.

O'Brien's had a lunch special: a free piece of Dentyne

with every pint so guys could return to work or to their wives smelling fresh and optimistic. The weather let up. I couldn't see it as much as I could tell by the sound—tires cutting a thinner skin of rain. Benny would be awake, his hands smoothing the girl's pale body. This thought made me want to run back to the motel and calmly explain to the blonde that Benny was mine. That his hands were mine, that his skin and nails and kidneys were mine. And then I would explain the same to Benny. I stared at the front door and downed my drink but it didn't give me the courage I needed. That was when Tati walked in.

Pink cowboy boots, a rabbit-fur coat, full waxy red lips.

"He's still alive if that's what you wanna know," Tati said, tossing her coat onto the bar and taking up the stool next to me.

Tati was Chinese, a real one from China, and the guys at the bar liked to call us twins because we were both skinny Orientals. Beyond that, we didn't look much alike. Her hair was short and punk with streaky bangs that sliced her forehead, all of this a contrast to her soft, heart-shaped face. My face was a block, and my hair was long and crooked because I chopped it myself with arts-and-crafts scissors. Tati hadn't been around in a while, so I was happy to see her, especially since she always had money.

"Am I in the papers yet?" she asked Henry, which made him chuckle and roll his cigar in his mouth. After ordering Baileys with whipped cream, she pulled out her rabbit's foot key chain from her skirt pocket and set it on the bar. Tati was the most superstitious person I'd ever met, always petting her rabbit's foot or handing out acorns to people having a bad day. She also placed an acorn on the counter after each drink until she had three. When ordering her fourth drink she'd shove all the acorns back into her pocket and start over because she avoided four of anything. Four was death.

Henry put her drink down. "So. You really toss a cleaver at your old man?"

From her coat pocket she whipped out a switchblade and opened it with a click. "Vinh gave it to me. Taught me how to throw it, too."

Tati then turned to me and explained that the cops had come out to her house the night before because she had thrown a knife at her father—all this over Vinh, a Vietnamese gangster the father had forbidden her to date. While Henry examined the knife, Tati poured a waterfall of sugar into her drink. A few sprinkles landed on the counter. She swept them onto her palm and threw a pinch over her shoulder.

"I thought you did that with salt," I said.

She clapped her hands clean. "Why take a chance."

"You hit the poor fuck with this?" Henry asked, still eyeing the silver blade.

"Just missed his ear. I killed the lampshade, though."

Henry laughed and looked to his buddies. "Little girls trying to whack their daddies. Ain't this a special time we're living in."

Tati's face changed. "I have an idea. Why don't you go give my dad a good fuck if you feel so bad for him."

Henry waved her away and went back to his pals without noticing the hurt in her voice. Or maybe he didn't care. Tati knocked on the counter three times before tucking her blade back into her pocket.

"You must really love Vinh," I said.

"Till the day I die," she said right away. "Till the day I die."

It hit me then that Tati—who acted so tough, who carried a knife and had a tattoo of a bleeding rose on the palm of her hand—was more innocent than I was, at least about love. Using the thin red straws as chopsticks, she scooped whipped cream into her mouth.

"I gotta make a call," she said, and hopped off the stool. She headed toward the back of the bar but paused in mid step. "Ah, fuck it," she said, and sat back down. She knocked wood three times again.

"You gain some weight?" she asked, patting my waist.

"No," I said, and took off a sweater.

"How many you got under there?"

I told her that I'd left Benny.

She slammed her hand on the counter, almost scaring me. "About fucking time," she hollered.

"I'm thinking of going back," I said. "You know, *make* him come to NA meetings with me."

She shook her head and took a drink. "You've said smarter things, little girl. Dating an addict when you're trying to quit has to be *the* stupidest thing."

Right up there with throwing a knife at your own father, I was tempted to say, but I knew it would hurt her feelings. I raised my glass to my lips only to find it empty.

"Maybe I can set you up with one of Vinh's friends," she said.

"Maybe you can buy me a drink," I said, and she did, after putting out an acorn for me.

By late afternoon, enough men had walked into O'Brien's to fill up every seat at the bar. They laughed and argued about football scores, whined about the rain, parking tickets, and the number 12 bus, which ran slower than Jimmy the retard, and oh shit, the old lady wants to celebrate another anniversary. Tati and I kept to ourselves at the end of the bar and drank like old men. We talked about our favorite songs and compared special names we were called in school for being Oriental. Chink. Gook. Chinky-chinky-ching-chong. She recounted all the bloody noses she'd handed out because of the teasing, and I imagined her beating up some of my own tormentors. But for the most part we talked about our dreams, like they really belonged to us, and as we drank, our imagined futures seemed as real and beautiful as the alcohol in our spines. I wanted a place of my own, with a mailbox and a toaster, but was too embarrassed to want something as ridiculous as love. She wanted money and to be a kindergarten teacher.

"You mean, like with kids?"

"What's the problem?" She looked hurt but sounded angry.

"Nothing. I'm just surprised."

"Hey." She punched my shoulder. "Look at me when you say that. Just because I'm a bitch doesn't mean I don't have feelings," she said, and knocked wood again.

"I'm sorry," I said. "But, you know..."

"What?"

I took a swig. "Your boyfriend's in a gang and you almost stabbed your father."

"That's right," she said, and held up an index finger. "Almost." Tati then shot up from her seat, saying she had to call Vinh. She straightened her skirt and walked toward the back. Before she could reach the hallway where the phone was, someone put a hand on her arm. It was the old man, the one with the dog in the basket. Henry was crouched behind the bar, changing a keg.

"Have you seen my Mary?" the old man asked, and without missing a beat, Tati pulled out a bill from her pocket and tucked it into the man's hand. "Take care of yourself, okay?" she said, and smoothed the dog's head before walking off. The old man stared at the money in his palm like he was waiting for it to speak.

"You gotta be fucking kidding me. You again!" Henry

screamed louder than I'd ever heard him, but my eyes stayed with Tati and her commanding stride toward the pay phone. Her love for Vinh seemed so simple, so determined. It burned me to watch her drop coins into the slot and press numbers she knew by heart. I thought about calling the motel. The pay phone there was by the manager's room, about three doors down from ours. Benny wouldn't hear it. At least not with the TV on. Plus, what would I say to him?

O'Brien's was busy now. The nighttime crowd had blown a canopy of smoke over the bar, over balding heads, curly heads, capped heads, and red heads. I noticed a guy. He was taller than the rest, his arms were titanic, and he looked like he ate bricks for breakfast. Nothing about him reminded me of Benny. He shot me a grin and I shot one back and slinked up to him, carefully anchoring one foot in front of the other. Then with all the sex in my voice, I placed a hand on his chest and asked if he wanted to buy me a drink.

He laughed and then I laughed, but then he laughed longer. "You're not exactly my type," he said, his eyes connecting with the eyes of his buddies.

I must've looked confused because he then said, "Your chest is too flat. You're not my type, okay?"

"Jesus, Joe. That's a little harsh," his friend said.

"Hey, I'm just being honest," the guy said, and they continued to discuss the value of honesty as though I weren't there.

I went back to my seat. My face felt gigantic. I wanted Tati to return so I wouldn't look so alone. Without thinking, and without looking at the guy, I played with Tati's rabbit's foot, stroking the creamy white fur with the back of my hand until I felt a distinct toenail. The foot was real—it had once been on a real rabbit. I pushed it away, but then took hold of it again, hoping that the creepy shiver running down my neck would maybe push out all other feelings. Tati returned. She grabbed the foot back.

"What took you so long?"

She stared silently at the sloping tower of pint glasses in front of us and rubbed her rabbit's foot as if trying to nurse it back to life. I asked if she was okay. She said she was, and to prove it, she ordered us another round. And I kept drinking because Tati kept buying and it was dark out now and Benny would be fucking.

"Fuck Benny," I said at some point in the night, holding up my scotch.

"Fuck men," Tati said, loud enough to get some looks.

"We're prettier than them, we're smarter than them. We're just better."

"Gooder," I said.

"Women are fucking perfect," she said.

"Perfect bitches!" a guy yelled.

"Who the fuck needs you?" Tati spat a wad of phlegm in the general direction of the voice and tapped me to do the same.

I searched my mouth. It was too cottony.

"I really mean it," she said in a whisper. "You're better than that."

I nodded. I wanted to lie down.

"I'm talking about you, stupid," she said, and smacked me across the face.

I grabbed my cheek and stretched my jaws. "Did you just slap me?"

"You know what you are?" she asked.

"Someone you just slapped?"

"You're a ball," she said.

"I'm a ball."

"You're the ball attached to the paddle, you know, the one with the rubber string."

"String," I said.

"The paddle beats up the ball but the ball keeps coming back."

"Sounds like fun," I told her. I didn't want to get into it.

She squeezed her face. "God. You're really dumb for
an Oriental," she said, and went on about how *her* boyfriend was a real man who didn't need drugs. "Vinh looks
out for me. He's got my back. Always."

I want to see your insides, Benny had said. We were high
on dust and he wanted to cut me open. We'd decided to
quit shooting up, so we test-drove every drug we could
find and found dust. When he said he wanted to cut
me, this seemed reasonable. That's what happens when
you smoke. You put that stem to your lips and the world
shrinks to a postcard. You see everything, all at once. You
understand the connections. The moon's a slice of salami.
Your mother's a ship. Lightbulbs and baby heads, honey-
dew and ladybugs. Knives and scabs and love. Everything
made sense. Benny made sense

"I want to cut you open," he said.

"I said yes already."

"Yeah, but I really want to."

"You want me to get the blade?" I asked.

"No. I think that should be my job. I don't want to be lazy about this." He rushed to the table by the window and rifled through our pile of pennies, cotton swabs, cans of chili, forks and knives and packets of oyster crackers. He came back to bed with a razor blade.

"Okay. Get on your back," he said, sitting up on his knees.

"You want to cut my stomach?"

"No. I'm sorry. Get on your stomach. I'll practice on your back first, and when I get better, then we can open up your front."

When I turned over I thought I might throw up. We had drunk almost a half a gallon of milk each to protect our stomach lining from the dust. I hated the taste of milk, so Benny mixed it with beer, and now I wanted to puke all over. But then he cut me, quickly, without warning, just below the right shoulder blade.

"Did you feel that?" he asked, his voice steady.

I told him I didn't, but really, I wasn't sure.

"How about this?" He made a second slice, slowly this time, along the left shoulder blade. I thought I could feel something hiss out of me.

"Am I bleeding?"

"Yeah." He stopped a trickle from sliding down my side. "You taste like raisins."

"Can you see anything?" I asked.

He got close, his breath warming the cuts. "I think you have wings."

"Doesn't everybody?" I said.

"Fuck…" he said, like a sigh. "Jesusfuckingchrist I love you so much." He laughed and kissed the back of my head. "Okay, okay," he said. "I need to focus." He splayed the cuts with his fingers and examined them, making little sounds of discovery. I asked him what he saw now.

"I think I see a bone."

"Okay," I said.

"I think I see a bone," he said again, as if saying it for the first time. He got up, almost tripped while stumbling to our table, and came back with a spoon. He jimmied the handle of the spoon into a cut until he found something he could tap.

"You hear that?" he asked.

I told him I did.

"What does it feel like?"

"Like you're tapping a bone in my body."

"I'm so glad this doesn't hurt. I don't want to hurt you."

"It doesn't hurt."

"Maybe this is your superhero power," he said. "Maybe you can't feel pain."

The mattress felt damp under my breasts. I wanted to turn over but I didn't think I should. I felt dizzy. "I don't feel good," I said.

"That's impossible. We just agreed that you didn't feel pain."

"I think I need a doctor."

"I am a doctor," he said, almost sounding hurt.

"I need a real one, someone with a stethoscope."

"Hold on. Wait here. I think I saw one in the trash can outside." Benny got up, got dressed, and said he'd be right back.

Weeks later, after stitches and bandages and scabs, Benny told this story to some people but ended it by saying it was his idea to get me to the hospital, not for my sake, but so he could steal a stethoscope. He never got the laugh he wanted.

O'Brien's turned empty. Behind the counter, Henry sat slumped on his stool with his arms crossed, asleep with the cigar in his mouth. His throat gurgled with every breath and raindrops ticked against the front door and Tati talked a string of ribbons, the words flowing so easily from her mouth, until at some point the alcohol in her decided that we needed to go to the Empire State Building. "C'mon!" she shouted. "We deserve to be on the top of the world!"

"I deserve a bed," I said. "I really feel like I should have one by now."

"I think it's got like five thousand floors," she said. "I read that somewhere."

"I want Benny. I want to smell him."

"I wanna stare down five thousand floors," she said.

We were nowhere near the Empire State Building but I put on my sweater and jacket and agreed to go because it was good to have a place to go. I knew that we'd never get there. I knew this, in the same way I knew that Tati would never be a teacher, and that Benny would be the end of me. Life's about confirming what we already know. About making sure. Didn't I know I'd go back to him that night and find him on the floor, shooting the girl up between her toes, between the one that went to the market and the one that stayed home, and didn't I know I would give up and give in? I knew. Henry knew. The man in the White Castle knew. Even the discount shoes and the plastic cakes and the blinking neon psychic knew.

Tati and I ran in the rain to catch up to the 12. With

her skipping over every single crack, especially in those cowboy boots of hers, we didn't have a chance. "Stop!" she shouted, but the bus was too far gone. "Goddamn it! I never have luck with buses!" she yelled, kicking a metal trash can by the bus stop. I thought that would be the end of it but she kicked the can again and again and bashed it down with her heels while screaming, "You fucking piece of shit!"

I wanted to tell her that people all over the world missed buses and she wasn't that special, but thought better of it. When I finally got her to leave the trash can alone she sat on the bus bench and knocked on it six times. I stayed standing. The rain came down hard, the drops sounding like marbles against the shelter's plastic. Across the street, people ducked under awnings or hopped into steamed-up cabs, and others ran past as if being chased by ghosts, newspapers and knapsacks roofing their heads. "Maybe it's just as well," I said. "I should get going anyway."

"Fine. Go. You got your free drinks." With her palms, she rubbed her eyes, trying to push the tears back in.

"What are you talking about?" I asked, even though I knew exactly what she meant.

"Forget it," she said. "I'm fine."

I couldn't face her. Down the block, a man stepped into a phone booth and shut the door, spraying a clean blue light onto the sidewalk, onto the rainwater gushing down Hemming Street, which now seemed as endless as the guilt I was feeling. I sat next to Tati. The rain had turned her hair into strands of black licorice.

"I just really wanted us at the Empire State Building, that's all."

I suggested we go tomorrow.

"It's no good tomorrow." She kicked a bottle cap into the street, where a car with duct-taped windows drove by. "I wanted to be up there tonight, above everything and everybody. Tonight."

I touched her shoulder and told her she wasn't making any sense.

She knocked my hand away. "This was something *I* wanted. Me. Things never work out for me." She took out her rabbit's foot. "I rub this thing a hundred fucking times and it doesn't do shit." She said this and tossed the foot, keys and all, into the middle of the street.

I wanted to understand her but it seemed easier to think of her as spoiled and melodramatic. And I would've kept that opinion of her if she hadn't told me that she'd been wanting to see the Empire State Building since she was eight, that she'd asked her father to take her but he had refused, saying she didn't deserve anything good. He'd said it just like that. Then Tati told me she was supposed to have been born a boy, and the boy was supposed to bring luck to her family. Her father had even changed her name from a girl's to a boy's, from Tai-shuan to Tai-shing, and he shaved her head and dressed her like a boy until she was seven. None of it worked.

"Every time something bad happened to the family, my father beat the shit out of me. That fucker used everything. Rocks. Belts. Shoes. Whatever he could get. And he blamed me for everything. If he lost his wallet, I got a beating. If he lost his job, I got a beating. When they had my sister, he beat the fuck out of me because she wasn't a boy. My parents had three more girls, so you do the math."

It killed me to hear her talk about her pain so easily, with something as simple as anger. It had never occurred to me that I could be angry with my parents, that I could yell at them or fight with them or even have thoughts of throwing knives at them.

"I just wanted things to be different today," she said. "I wanted to see that stupid building. And I wanted to see Vinh and tell him that I would've killed my father for him. Vinh's the one good thing that's ever happened to me, the only person that's ever loved me, and that fucker can't stand it because I finally got something good and his life's still shit."

Tati stopped talking and I didn't know how to make her feel better. So I reminded her to knock on wood.

"Thanks." She knuckled the bus bench twenty-three times. It took a while.

The rain kept falling and I felt as though bits of me were falling with it. I was tired and the booze was wearing off, just enough to remind me that Benny was in a motel room that I'd paid for, losing himself to a girl who didn't deserve to see him lost.

"Hey, if you ever want me to go to those NA meetings with you, I'll go," she said.

I told her thanks.

"And if you need a place to crash, just say so, okay? You don't need that scumbag."

I ran my hand along the bottom of the bench and tried to feel all the dings and divots. I wanted that scumbag.

"That's disgusting."

It took me a second to realize Tati wasn't talking about me. She was looking down the block, past the pay phone. It was the old man. With his legs apart, he was crouching over the gutter and washing his face in rainwater, his ears and neck, too.

"I bet you it's some girlfriend," Tati said.

The old man stopped washing and reached into the water. I thought I saw him fish something out and place it in his basket but I couldn't see what. "What girlfriend?"

"This Mary he's looking for. I bet she's from a long time ago, like when he was a kid, some girl he would've died for but he let life and bullshit get in their way."

"Mary could be a dog," I said.

"It could be, but it's not. Only love makes you run around in the rain without feeling cold. Only love numbs you out like that and still lets you feel every fucking cell in your body." When Tati said this the look in her eyes told me that she was proud to have said it.

She stood up suddenly. "I gotta make a call."

I asked her who she was calling this late, even though I knew.

"I paged him like fifty times today."

"That's kind of sweet," I said, sincerely.

"He hasn't called back."

I looked at the ground. I felt too weak for this kind of honesty.

"I think he's fucking around on me." She looked out onto the street in front of us as if it were the ocean.

"Has he cheated before?"

"Nah," she said, walking away. "But with my luck."

The rain finally slowed. For a second I felt lucky. At least Benny cheated in front of me. A strong wind played with the row of traffic lights, and the old man, who was now a few blocks away, looked like an old thought. Across the street a bus pulled up. People got off and rushed into a dive bar with a blinking martini. I could hear laughter coming from there and, if I strained enough, music from a jukebox. The melody, low and muted, made me want to head back to the motel, get back under the covers. I'd been away from him maybe twenty hours now and I missed him needing me, I missed him looking at me. Benny had round, wishful eyes, and he wanted everything from me. And when I gave him everything and was left with nothing, he wanted that, too. He was always hungry. His body was a long white candle of wax and bones, and he was always hungry. If that wasn't love, I didn't know what was. While Tati was in the phone booth, praying for the phone to ring, I got up and left for the motel. I didn't say goodbye. I didn't even turn around to see if she could see me leave. What did I know about love and fate and fortune back then? These were big words and you could only gain their meaning if you looked up at the sky but I could only look down and see myself in the wet grains of cement, in the cracks, in the moss that grew between the cracks.

A year later I saw Tati for the last time, in prison. She was in not for killing her father but her boyfriend Vinh. That night, after I left, Tati walked over to his place. He wasn't home but a neighbor woman told her that she had bumped into Vinh as he and his sister were entering an all-night movie theater. Tati didn't bother telling the woman that Vinh was an only child. She ran to the theater and found him sitting in the front row, finger-fucking some girl. Tati took out her switchblade and waved it at the girl, scream-ing, kicking, promising her the worst death imaginable.

Through the pellet-sized holes of the Plexiglas win-dow, Tati told me that she had only wanted to scare the slut but that Vinh stepped in between them. He turned toward her and caught the knife between his ribs.

"I really loved him," she said, almost a whisper.

"I know," I told her.

The guard tapped on the door behind her, signaling for us to wrap it up. Tati rubbed the top of her head, which was now shaved.

"What do you think the odds are of someone dying from a switchblade wound?" she asked me.

I said that I didn't know.

".058," she said.

I couldn't think of anything to say but that number rang in my ears for days.

"I guess it was meant to be," she said, not necessarily to me.

At the
Employment Agency

The nameplate on his desk read Ted Flukinjer, Recruiter. A small wiry man with no arm hair, he shrugged behind a large metal desk, a pencil poised over an open file folder. My folder. I crossed my legs and hoped for him to peer up, just once, to see how professional I looked in a blouse and skirt. I kept my briefcase on my lap, and even though it was empty, except for my seven dollars and a stick of gum, the weight of it calmed my knees. I fixed my skirt and straightened my stockings. Mr. Flukinjer himself wore a short-sleeved shirt and tie. It was a clip-on. I knew this because the beak of his collar was flipped up, unveiling nothing but the yellow of his shirt.

"Are you eighteen or over?"

"Yes," I said, and for once I wasn't lying.

"Previous work experience."

"Yes."

"I'm asking you to name where you've worked."

"Oh. I could just—"

"For example, have you worked in customer service, retail, commercial offices, or in the health industry."

I nodded but he still had his head down, so I said yes, maybe too loudly. He pencil-checked a box.

"Start with the most current."

"I worked in a nursing home."

"Position held."

"I was the assistant to the activities director."

"Reason for leaving."

"I got fired."

He paused his pencil. With a look of restrained disgust, he jerked his head to the right, as if my answer had slapped him in the face. He sighed through his nose.

"Reason for termination."

"I stole from them."

He tapped the pencil on the desk to the pace of a ticking time bomb. Still, he wouldn't look up.

"I'm sorry. My NA sponsor told me I should be honest about my past. All the time, to everyone."

"What's NA?" he asked a stapler to his left.

"Narcotics Anonymous."

"Great." He pronounced and then noted "drug addict" into my file.

"Recovering," I corrected him. "It sounds nicer."

"Any arrests."

"Yes."

"Wonderful."

"Just misdemeanors."

"Plural. Excellent. You drive?"

"No."

"Experience with a ten-key."

"Is that a calculator?"

"If you have to ask, you don't know it. Next. Can you take dictation, I'm going to answer that for you and check no. Operate a switchboard, again a no. Can you type?" The pencil tip hovered over the no box, waiting for my answer.

I thought about the typing class I'd taken in seventh grade.

"Yes." I cleared my throat. "Definitely."

"Oh really," he said, facing me squarely. Flat brows, tidy nose, coffee teeth. The orbs of his eyes, enormous and white, showed too much anatomy. "How fast?"

At the Employment Agency

. . .

After four practice tests, he clocked me at seventeen words per minute, as long as numbers, punctuation, and capital letters weren't involved.

We were back at his desk.

"Okay, so that's a no on typing." He checked off the final box and gave my application the once-over, signed, stapled, and rubber-stamped the bottom of pages like a machine set to HI. When he finished he shut my folder and laid his pencil gently on top of it, as if placing a pea there. I played with a button on my blouse.

"This can't be news to you…" He leaned back on his chair and interlocked his fingers before resting them on his stomach. "You didn't do so hot here."

"I know." I sat up on the edge of my seat. "What can we do about it?"

"*We* aren't doing anything. You're not hirable, plain and simple. With your record, lack of experience, no high school education. Nobody's going to want you, and that's the truth."

"Oh." I put my briefcase down, hadn't realized I'd been holding it the entire time. I could feel tears welling up in my eyes, so I bit the inside of my lips, a new and beautiful habit of mine. It seemed stupid to cry there, in that office, after all I'd been through.

"I understand," I said, nodding.

"Good." He pushed my folder to the side and picked up the receiver. "Now, if you don't mind, I have to . . ."

"I understand," I said again, barely able to say the words this time.

"Good luck to you." He got up to shake my hand except I didn't move. "I have to make a call and that means you have to go now."

"I understand," I said, for the third time, unable to stop my head from nodding. I grabbed my briefcase, and I did plan to get up and go but some force pushed the briefcase to my chest and made me say out loud: "I can't leave. You have to give me something. Anything."

He rolled his eyes. "Oh God, not again," he grumbled, and sat back down, the phone still in his grip. He shook his head at the door, which was open, the sounds of conversations drifting in and out.

"Look." I stood up and put a hand on his desk. "I've sobered up. I'm clean. I was an A student. I'm smart, I'm hardworking. I can play the piano, I can clean houses, or pick up trash. I don't care. Just try me out, for one week."

He applauded. "Are you finished?"

"Depends."

"I'm sorry your life was so tragic but, really, I don't have time for it right now. So if you want to sit there and pout, suit yourself." He pulled out a Rolodex from one of his drawers and spun it to a card. "We all have problems," he said, and dialed a number.

"I think you're making a big mistake," I said, sitting back down.

For about an hour I listened to him make several more calls. My briefcase and I didn't budge, and Mr. Flukinjer went about his business. Too easily, I thought. He made a call to someone who annoyed him, saying things like, "That's not what we agreed on," and "That's a complete lie." Then he called his son, whom he called "buddy" and "pal" while promising to take him to Playland. A few calls were made about an apartment rental, and finally a call about a new set of tires for his '77 Chevy Impala. Office workers came in once in a while to drop off paperwork or to ask him questions, and if anyone said hi to me he'd say, "Don't mind her," and wave their attention back to him.

Another hour went by, during which he found jobs for other people. After delivering the good news, he would end the phone conversation with, "Good. I'm glad it worked out," and sneak a peek at my reaction.

During these calls something bulky settled in my gut, the weight of it keeping me down. I realized then that I wasn't being brave by not leaving his office—I was simply sinking. Into the chair, into the past, where images of Jake the night manager at the Plaza Motel came to me. He had taken my money without letting me and Lana stay in that room, and I had given up too easily. I should've fought harder. That was my money. But instead I left that lobby, like I'd left everything else in my life. My home, my mother, my name. Leaving was all I knew. That was all I was qualified for.

I looked up at Mr. Flukinjer. He looked too tired for me to hate him. The baggy folds under his eyes tried to drag the rest of his face down. His office had one window and the light from it had darkened to a sooty gray. Coworkers poked in and gave their goodnights, the air conditioner fell silent. Placing his briefcase on his desk, he slowly and gently clicked open the latches, letting me know with some sympathy that my time was up. He began packing, sliding folders and pens into their rightful pockets. I stared blankly at his hands, waiting to see what they would look like clasping the briefcase shut. He pulled out a sandwich, wrapped in clear plastic, to make room for a binder.

"You hungry?" he whispered, and that was what unraveled me. The way he barely said the words. The way he looked at me without looking at me. The way he held the sandwich so hesitantly, wanting me to take it but not wanting to offend, understanding that even someone like me could have pride. All I remember is my face against his chest, the smell of pencils, and him holding me the way a father would, stroking my head and saying things I hadn't heard before. I knew I was crying. The sounds were definitely coming from my chest, though I didn't recognize myself in them. When my sobbing slowed, Mr. Flukinjer let go and sat me back down. He got me a glass of water, for himself, too, and wheeled his chair around so we could be on the same side of his desk. There, listening to the hum that follows a burst of emotions, we sat on the edges of our seats and shared the sandwich.

"How are you at math?" he asked.

I broke off a corner of the bread and whispered into the tear, "I'm Korean, so..."

"Right," he said, and gave a short laugh, erasing the pity that was poisoning the air.

. . .

I had gone into the employment agency with seven dollars and a stick of gum, and came out five hours later with a job delivering lunches to offices. It paid $3.35 an hour, plus a free lunch if there was a mistake in ordering. Three-thirty-five times eight hours a day is $26.80. Times that by five days a week and you get $134, and $134 multiplied by 52 weeks is $6,968, which meant that I could get an apartment with a mailbox and a toaster, and maybe within a year I could have enough money to move to California, where the sun was free for anyone who wanted it.

It took two people to deliver these lunches. One to drive and wait in the truck, and one to enter the offices and hand out the meals. I was that person.

Mr. McCommon

Long before I moved out to California. Long before I caught Wink on the evening news, talking about how glad he was for having finally contracted HIV so he could be hospitalized and cared for like the people he'd seen on the news. Long before Knowledge got clean and got work as a counselor in a teen shelter, only to be shot by a kid she was trying to help out.

Long before all this.

I returned to my mother's house in the Bronx. I wanted proof that she had not been a ghost, that she had been as real as blood.

On my way there I pictured our place—a two-story tract home that held down the corner before the ground swelled to a small, grassy hill that lipped the expressway.

Cars were always leaving us. Only a few trickled down the exit ramp, and I could hear the sputtering of engines from my bedroom, late at night, when the silence after my parents fought kept me numb and awake. I figured that another family might be living there now, lounging around as if the living room, the vegetable garden, and the front windows bleached by the three o'clock sun had always been theirs. But when I stood at the end of my block I saw no family. And I barely recognized the house. In all the years of reimagining my childhood home, not once had I pictured it boarded up and abandoned.

All the windows were nailed with plywood, and the screen door lay crooked on top of a sagging hedge. Bands of graffiti blackened the aluminum siding, even the dead, brittle lawn, and someone had spray-painted NZONE on the front door, vertically, one letter stacked neatly on top of the other. I couldn't help but take all of it personally. I was being punished for having left without looking back. Five years had gone by, though judging by the sickly roof, the derailed gutters, and the detached emptiness I felt about my mother's death, it might as well have been five light-years.

I walked to the rear, where the kitchen door stood unfazed by all the garbage surrounding it—beer cans, a single flip-flop, a plastic grocery bag trapped under a can of Valvoline. Without much hope I jiggled the brassy doorknob. Nothing. I even tried the back basement door, the one my father had used to escape in the middle of the night to see his mistress, until my mother suddenly took an interest in carpentry and nailed the door shut with two-by-fours, from both inside and out. In return, my father nailed up her dresser drawer, just the top one, where she kept her Bible and brown photos of herself as a ponytailed girl in Korea. This was how my parents talked. They used nails, hammers, dinner plates, and knives, and when those didn't work, they used leaving.

I circled the house. The plank on the side kitchen window—the same one I had once peeked through to see my mother rising from the ground—looked especially warped. I marked a mental X in the center, backed up a few steps, braced my arm and charged, leading with a shoulder and channeling all the TV cops I'd seen doing this very maneuver. The cops were the size of a duplex and I was all of 105 pounds, but I hurled my body into the wood anyway—one, two, three times too many. A strong breeze had a better chance. Without screaming, I held the pain in my shoulder and understood what it was trying to tell me: that I was a stupid girl, that I wasn't getting into the house unless I got rid of my stupidity, and that I would never understand my mother.

"Joon, is that you?"

I was startled to find a man behind me. He was in his mid-fifties and nearly bald, with a few scraggly curls frizzying the sides. I had barely known Mr. McCommon when I was growing up, but he came in for a hug, which would've been fine except that I hadn't expected it. Our clumsy dance led to a sideways embrace, ending with a stutter of pats on the back. His tracksuit, a neon-green, felt both scratchy and smooth.

"I can't believe you're back," he said, and I kept my head down so he could study me without feeling awkward. "I thought you were dead."

A fly landed on his fresh white sneaker. "I thought I was dead, too," I told him.

The boys in the neighborhood had always made fun of his name—Mr. McCommon. Mr. McAverage. Mr. Mc-Usual. It didn't help that he'd worn a boring gray suit and tie almost every day and drove a car the color of masking tape. He was short and thin with narrow shoulders and a long forehead. The expression on his face, which was also long, reminded me of chalkboard that had just been erased—you knew something had lived there once but you never knew what. I'd always felt a little sympathy for him, maybe because the kids who made fun of him had also changed my name to Joon Ching-chong, Joon Ah-so, Joon Chow-mein. None of the kids cracked jokes about his wife, though, a woman everyone thought was the life of the neighborhood, with her frilly voice and large, blond hair. But to me, she was worse than the kids. Whenever my parents battled, I could always count on seeing Mrs. McCommon by her kitchen window, talking into the phone with a hand cupping her mouth, squinting at our house to get the play-by-play.

"Is Mrs. McCommon home?" I asked.

We were in his garage, looking for tools to pry open the plywood.

"No," he said, rummaging through a metal chest. "She had cancer."

He spoke casually, as if reading off a grocery list. I didn't know what to say.

"It's okay," he added. "She's not dead."

I halfheartedly sifted through an open cardboard box. "Is she all right?"

From the chest he pulled out a hammer and pondered

its dimensions. "She's probably fine," was all he said, and I let his answer be.

The front half of the garage was a jumble of boxes, laundry baskets, and crates. Some mounds reached my waist and none were labeled or in any way organized. The rear of the garage was a different story. A skyline of neatly stacked items almost eclipsed the entire back wall—items I didn't think anyone collected. Like the white foam trays that come with supermarket meat. Or bundles of old newspaper, every single one wrapped in the Sunday comics. Or empty boxes of Kleenex. Slouching in a corner were roughly twenty paper bags, all of them labeled and brimming with throwaways, like lightbulbs, blue plastic razors, curled tubes of toothpaste, and—maybe the most confusing—clumps of used tissue. That every item was categorized and kept so tidy was what stunned me.

I turned around. Mr. McCommon was still on his knees, now leaning over a different box. His jacket was open, and poking up from an interior pocket was a pudgy cream-colored envelope, the return address inked in calligraphy. It seemed on the verge of falling out, not that he noticed. An orange work light hooked to a beam tanned the crown of his head while blurring his face in shadow, but I could still make out the absolute determination in his eyes. And in his arms, which were elbow-deep in the box, swirling items around in a mad search. Why he was so set on helping me I didn't know. Maybe he didn't, either. I picked a crate and started digging. I wanted to ask why he saved the things he saved but figured that if I felt uneasy asking, then he'd feel uneasy answering. I instead asked if he knew what had happened to all of our stuff.

"The bank foreclosed on your house. I'm guessing they sold everything."

I flipped through an old magazine. "I wonder what they got for my junior-high yearbook."

He laughed through his teeth.

"What am I looking for again?" I asked.

"A crowbar, or anything that behaves like a crowbar."

My hands touched tangled stockings, tubes of lipstick, a blond wig, empty tubs of Noxzema, and other remains, but nothing resembling a tool.

"Mr. McCommon?"

"Yes."

"Can I ask you a question?"

"Here, slide that over," he said, pointing to a laundry basket filled with a hodgepodge of blankets and batteries and music boxes. I nudged it over with my foot.

"How do you remember us?"

"What do you mean?"

"My mother and me. What did we look like to you?"

Without looking up he said, "Troubled. Just like everybody else."

"You and Mrs. McCommon always seemed—"

"Goddamn it!" He chucked something back into the basket and stood up. "I know I have a crowbar somewhere in here." With hands on hips, he looked down the driveway and shook his head as if disagreeing with the trash cans sitting by the curb. The clouds hung low, and the sun was failing. Across the street, a porch light blinked twice before coming on, and that slight hesitation made me wonder if I should leave. The dust in the garage powdered my throat, and plus, I didn't think I needed to see the dying insides of my childhood home. Some things were best kept in the dark. Like my past. Like Mr. McCommon's collections.

"Try over there." Mr. McCommon pointed to a skinny workbench that stood against the right side of the garage. Blue milk crates took up most of the counter. One was filled with kitchen utensils. Another a mayhem of hairbrushes, combs, a blow-dryer, leather gloves, and a pocket-sized Bible, the same kind my mother had kept in her purse. A lime-green pleather cover with *The New Testament* inscribed in gold. The color matched Mr. McCommon's tracksuit, and it came to me then that I'd never seen him in anything but gray. I picked up the mini Bible, opened to a page to smell it but the scent didn't remind me of my mother's hand cream.

"Finally." Mr. McCommon stood behind me, holding a crowbar as if it were a torch. "Come on. Let's go break into your house."

The moon was full, its light widening the sky around it. Mr. McCommon carried the hammer and the crowbar. I carried a flashlight. The neighborhood was quiet; *he* was quiet. I could hear the scrapes of his tracksuit and the long, distant sighs of the expressway as we drifted across my mother's driveway, her yard, and faced the kitchen window.

"Stand back," he said, pushing up his sleeves. At the lower right side of the plywood, he wedged in the flat end of the crowbar and started hammering it in. "I can't see," he said, and I aimed the flashlight at his hands. With a third of the rod now jammed behind the wood, he dropped the hammer, gripped and re-gripped the crook of the crowbar, braced his foot against the aluminum siding, and pulled. "I remember when the workers boarded up the house," he said, grunting with every effort.

"Do you want some help?"

"They didn't mess around." He looked like he was being strangled, the flesh around his eyes and mouth ballooning.

"I can pull with you, if you want."

"Big . . . guys, with big . . . nail guns." He changed to an underhanded grip and planted his foot higher on the siding. "But this crowbar . . . should do the trick." He growled and pulled with renewed strength but the plywood budged less than an inch.

"Maybe we shouldn't be doing this," I said.

"Why not." He hammered in the crowbar farther. "Sometimes it's good to break the rules. Let the neighbors call the cops, I don't care." He yanked harder, and this time his arms began to tremble. I thought they might pop off.

I hadn't even thought about the neighbors. "Don't hurt yourself."

He gritted his teeth, his face frozen in pain, and then as if the sound had been boiling in his stomach for years, he let out a scream so loud and so long, I was sure he'd grown another vocal cord.

"Goddamn it!" he screamed, and picked up the hammer, held it like an ax, and for reasons unclear to me, he began clobbering the wood.

"Mr. McCommon?"

"Not now!" he barked. He was exploding. His arms swung wildly above his head though his face appeared to be doing all the work. Deep, guttural sounds spilled from his crooked lips with every slam, but as wild as his strokes were, the plywood didn't give. "Son of a bitch," he mumbled, and swung harder, out of control. The sound of metal whacking wood struck my temples.

"We really don't have to do this," I told him.

"—Yes

"—I

"—do," he said, and delivered maybe five more swings, each one making a crescent-shaped dimple, each one slowing the next one down, until he finally and simply released the hammer, the head thudding the ground. He folded his body, his palms clutched his thighs, and with every gasp his chest whistled.

"Are you okay?"

"Am I okay?" He laughed, maybe for too long, and the sheer frustration of his laughter clung to my skin. He slumped to the ground, leaned back against the aluminum siding, and closed his eyes. "She said I was boring."

I turned the flashlight off and sidled up next to him.

"I'm the one who watched her going bald. I changed her sheets when she couldn't get to the bathroom in time. I fed her Jell-O, I drained her bedsores. I'm the one who gave her sponge baths. Me. And after all that, she says I'm too dull."

From where we sat, we could see the orange, square glow that came from his garage.

"She didn't want to die married to me."

"But she didn't die," I said.

"Now she's marrying some merchant marine."

"But she's still alive," I said, as loud as I had intended. When the words left me, all I wanted was to run to his garage, pull down the door, bury myself under batteries and blankets and lipsticks and rubber bands, and sleep inside his city of remains.

"I'm sorry about your mother," he whispered.

I felt a tiny collapsing in my chest and it took me a moment to correctly identify the pang, not as grief, but as jealousy. I hadn't loved my mother the way he had loved his wife. I had left her when she needed me most, and in the end, she died, in a car, completely alone with nothing but the sound of metal crushing her. I couldn't grieve for her, not because I didn't want to, but because I didn't deserve to. I looked at Mr. McCommon, his hands smothering his face, his chest flinching. He had no idea that grief was a reward. That it only came to those who were loyal, to those who loved more than they were capable of. He had a garage, full of her belongings, and all I had was my guilt. It took on its own shape and smell and nestled in the pit of my body, and it would sleep and play and walk with me for decades to come.

For a long while we stayed just as we were, listening to the air, letting the expressway mourn our loss. I asked if I could take the green pocket-sized Bible.

"I still miss her," he said, like he was breathing, and I didn't have the heart to repeat myself.

And then, without discussion, we both stood up and tried the window again. Between the two of us, it took just a few minutes to pry off a corner of the wood, only to discover that another plank was boarding up the window from the inside. We never got in, and somehow that seemed appropriate. On our way back to his garage, Mr. McCommon looked up at his bedroom window, which was dark like the rest of his house. "I even miss seeing her sick," he said, and that seemed to me a truth I could hold on to about my mother, a place to begin.

Acknowledgments

For their monumental support, I would like to thank the Norton Island Residency, MacDowell Colony, Corporation of Yaddo, Key West Literary Seminar, Tin House Summer Writers Workshop, Squaw Valley Community of Writers, Hopwood Awards Committee, and the University of Michigan MFA program, where I was fortunate to be mentored by the ridiculously generous Peter Ho Davies, Eileen Pollack, Michael Byers, and Nick Delbanco.

I am in awe of my editor, Megan Lynch, and my agent, Amy Williams. Their unflagging commitment to this book feels more like love than business. My gratefulness to Barney Rosset, Julie Barer, P. J. Mark, Jim Houston, Lee Montgomery, Alex Chee, Steve McManus, Bonnie Maliler, Tom Farber, Sandra Gilbert, Marcela Valdes, Rachel Kash, Oyamo, Margaret Dean, Chris Hebert, and all my mates at the University of Michigan. Thanks also to the gang at Schmidt's Tobacco Trading Co. & Pub for always saving a seat for me and my laptop. Special gratitude to

Acknowledgments

Kevin Jones for years of insightful feedback, and to Mitchell and Lucia Rose for loving me like a daughter.

The (Ashby Avenue) Groop gave me what every writer needs: other writers to admire and learn from. I feel especially indebted to John Beckman, Andy Berry, MJ Deery, Jen Deitz, Christian Divine, Bridget Hoida, Marco and Megan Morrone, Nick Petrulakis, and Jenn Stroud, who have read, reread, and argued about nearly every story in this book.

And most of all, my love and gratitude to Augustus Rose for never refusing a late-night "emergency" reading.

And to my sister, whose love can't be translated into words.

"Shelter" first appeared in *Witness*, and then in *Pushcart Prize XXXI*. "Club Orchid" first appeared, in different form, in *Evergreen Review*. "On the Bus" first appeared in *The Iowa Review*. "With a Boy" (formerly "Blue Fly") appeared, in different form, in *Tin House*. "What We Had" (formerly "Year of the Fire Dragon") first appeared, in different form, in *Eleven Eleven*.

The author gratefully acknowledges permission to quote from "Notes Towards a Poem That Can Never Be Written" by Margaret Atwood, from Selected Poems II: Poems Selected and New, 1976–1986 © 1981, 1987 by Margaret Atwood (U.S., Houghton Mifflin Co.); Selected Poems 1966–1984 © 1981, 1990 by Margaret Atwood (Canada, McClelland & Stewart Ltd.); Eating Fire: Selected Poetry 1965–1995 © 1998 by Margaret Atwood (UK, Virago Press).